WEAVERS *of* DESTINY

KATHY KNOWLTON

CANADA USA SPAIN UK IRELAND

Cover design by Olivia Zapata

Note for Librarians: a cataloguing record for this book that includes Dewey Decimal Classification and US Library of Congress numbers is available from the Library and Archives of Canada. The complete cataloguing record can be obtained from their online database at:
www.collectionscanada.ca/amicus/index-e.html
ISBN 1-4120-4382-4

TRAFFORD

Offices in Canada, USA, Ireland, UK and Spain
This book was published on-demand in cooperation with Trafford Publishing. On-demand publishing is a unique process and service of making a book available for retail sale to the public taking advantage of on-demand manufacturing and Internet marketing. On-demand publishing includes promotions, retail sales, manufacturing, order fulfilment, accounting and collecting royalties on behalf of the author.
Book sales for North America and international:
Trafford Publishing, 6E–2333 Government St.,
Victoria, BC V8T 4P4 CANADA
phone 250 383 6864 (toll-free 1 888 232 4444)
fax 250 383 6804; email to orders@trafford.com
Book sales in Europe:
Trafford Publishing (UK) Ltd., Enterprise House, Wistaston Road Business Centre, Wistaston Road, Crewe, Cheshire CW2 7RP UNITED KINGDOM
phone 01270 251 396 (local rate 0845 230 9601)
facsimile 01270 254 983; orders.uk@trafford.com
Order online at:
www.trafford.com/robots/04-2190.html

10 9 8 7 6 5 4 3 2

After the consolidation of communication among the many worlds and the establishment of the Interplanetary Authority as a trusted liaison, there arose a common desire to celebrate and demonstrate the achievement of this unprecedented interconnectedness. The Interspecies Games resulted, providing the first opportunity for many to become aware of the vast numbers of cooperative and mutually beneficial relationships among different species throughout the galaxy. A general success, the games not only continued at the now familiar interval, but also created change and unforeseen effects on many of the worlds involved. No event was more influential in this regard than the freestyle. In this event no set patterns or parameters such as speed or distance governed performances. Rather the species pairs demonstrated their ability to synchronize using naturally occurring behavior in keeping with their own cultures. Some analysts have speculated that this level of freedom contributed to the catalytic power freestyle teams appeared to exercise on their various planets.

Targall's *History of Cooperation*

Table of Contents

I

Jula And Her Blues

JULA SLAMMED her fist on the communicator control pad. "I know it's 'not sustainable' to transport me to the port, but the planet doesn't care! The planet wants us to go to the games!" Her blues fluttered around her just off her skin to avoid her turmoil.

The machine's flat voice responded. "This communicator does not tolerate violence. Functioning will stop." It managed to sound offended despite its lack of inflection. The tone signaling shutdown chimed. Jula sighed deeply and as she exhaled the swarm of deep blue butterflies always with her settled on her skin like a garment.

By herself she looked like what she was, a young female human – brown hair, green eyes, five feet four inches, sixteen years, a trifle skinny, but athletic. The blues gave her an off-earth otherness, particularly since she now rarely wore any clothing and simply let them cover her.

Her parents and the rest of that generation which had settled this lush green planet did not approve. Her mother had explained honestly. "They think there's something kind of sexual about it, having all those insects crawling all over you all the time." Jula had just rolled her eyes at this misunderstanding. How could she even begin to explain? It was easier sometimes, like now, to wear minimal underthings and not have to think about what they were thinking.

Far from disapproving, Jula's peers half-envied her. Indigenous animals had adopted about a third of the humans born since arrival, but most seemed familiar, like peculiarly inseparable pets. Only a few of the teenagers had anything as exotic as Jula's blues.

Jula sighed again. Her parents would be home soon from their work governing the settlements. She wished for the zillionth time that she had little brothers and sisters running around the house, even one, anybody to take some of the attention away from her. She loved her parents, really she did. It's just that they were all so close to each other, it made her want not to have any family at all. Her blues fluttered above her skin again in troubled eddies.

"You're right. We should just go practice," she said. Unseen in the next room her mother, Rula, knew Jula was addressing the butterflies as if they understood. Rula watched the girl slide open the transparent outer wall and run out into the mossy back yard surrounded by impenetrably thick jungle.

Jula started her dance silently, following a beat so clear that anyone watching could imagine music. Rula loved her daughter's talent. It always thrilled her to watch. The blues danced, too, extending beyond stretched hands, accentuating the long arch of a leg, floating like a scarf, like a skirt, rising in a high collar behind her head. Rula didn't mind how inhuman it looked, though she knew everyone else would. No, not inhuman , she corrected her thought. More ahuman, she decided, as if they, or this new planet, were creating a new intelligent species. How different would she be from her own grandchildren? Her husband sighed behind her.

"I love to watch her, but it makes me feel…distant from her, too," Drake confided. Rula nodded but neither turned from the mesmerizing view as they spoke.

"Each time I see this piece she's made it harder." She sounded awestruck. "There are places where the blues make her leaps larger. They actually hold her up."

Rula's joy and excitement radiated out from her, and Drake was certainly aware of how she felt, but no matter how he tried he couldn't join her in those feelings. His daughter's singlemindedness had always loomed like a barrier to him, even though Rula had made it quite clear she considered the trait a direct inheritance from him. He sighed. He felt obscurely that there was something unfair about his daughter's attitude toward him. Weren't adolescent girls supposed to find fault with their strong mothers rather than resisting their fathers? When he finally spoke, Drake's voice was tight. "She wants to try out for those interspecies games. She knows getting her off-planet requires a non-sustainable use of resources."

Rula had been looking for an opening to talk about this. "If we and three other families pledged our energy for this orbit, we could send her to the port."

"And then swelter during the rains." But he was considering it. "Anyway, how would she get off the planet? The whole bipedal population doesn't have enough allotment for interstellar travel."

"Bipedal?! You sound like a strict assimilationist. Next thing I know you'll be telling me we should give up our house and let Jula disappear into the jungle."

This elicited a grunt of disgust from Drake. His leadership of the factions grew harder by the month. The settlement party remained the majority, but the strict assimilationists were growing and inevitably the tiny separatist movement grew, too. Perhaps because they had few natural enemies on this benign world, the humans had turned more quickly against each other than was usual on a newly inhabited planet.

The dance had grown faster and faster. Now Jula did a series of fouettes that seemed to spin the blues upward centrifugally in a cloud, revealing her long legs and hiding the rest of her completely. She stopped and the blues kept flying wider and higher, as if they might disperse. Suddenly she and they collapsed into a tight crouch. She must have her arms around her knees and her head bent forward. They couldn't really tell, because the blues covered her completely. Nothing human showed. When the butterflies stirred again, perhaps they would reveal empty space where Jula had been. Perhaps they had managed to steal her away.

Slowly the blues began to peel back and up. Jula rose as if they were stretching her upright. The blues formed small patches where modesty would demand, but the rest of the swarm gathered in two forms behind her back. They and she seemed to uncurl forever. She held her arms high and looked up as the butterflies made deep blue wings twice her height. They flapped once, twice, and Jula rose from the ground. Her parents gasped. This they had never seen. This had no link for them to anything of earth. Jula looked down from where she hovered about twenty feet in the air and gestured as if to bless all below. Then, as slowly as they had unfurled, the blues lowered her and flowed into place as a dress.

Drake broke the silence inside the house. “At the meeting this morning Torval told me his boy has disappeared – you know, the kid with the riverdog. Only twelve. I felt like locking Jula up. Now I half wish I could send her off-planet, get her away from this place before she’s not our daughter any more.”

“We are settlers, my love. The generational divides are always magnified for the first few sets of people in a new world.” Rula knew what she said was true. She knew how close she felt to Jula, yet she felt a deep aching sympathy for this man she loved. And she fought to remain open to him without responding fearfully herself.

“Generational divides!” He hissed. “Sometimes I feel this place has paired up with our kids just to steal them from us.” She heard a hatred in his voice she had never experienced with him in the two decades of their marriage.

“Drake! You sound so threatened! None of the kids has been hurt. They’ve just assimilated. They’d be back and forth visiting all the time, if they trusted us to let them come and go.”

“They’re feral, Rula! Living like animals.”

Jula reentered the room. “We <u>are</u> animals. All of us. And they’re not ‘feral.’ You know I hate that word.”

“Did you know about Torval’s boy?” Drake accused more than asked.

“What if I did? It’s not as if I don’t think about it, too, you know. If it weren’t for the tryouts…”

“No!” Drake exploded. “You are not leaving this settlement.”

“What’s the matter with you?” Rula asked in astonishment. “You were just saying you wish she could go.”

“Please, Daddy. Just get me to the tryouts. The New Planet Fund will send me to the games if I qualify. I bet they will. They have scholarships for everything. Please?”

“No! You are not leaving this settlement.” Drake roared.

Jula moved toward the outside wall. “Oh, yes, we are.” She made the words as steely as she could, slid open the panel and ran.

Rula yelled as if she had been stabbed. “Jula! Please! Come back.” But the parents could do nothing except watch as Jula and her blues disappeared into the jungle at the edge of their yard.

II

Josh And Cor

On the planet Ayr light years away another mother, Audra, shivered as she recalled her own helpless watching. It had been soon after they moved into the warren of Cavernhome and she wasn't yet used to the stone walls and floors and ceilings everywhere. She had felt cold and she remembered taking her husband Jeb's hand and being glad when he held tight to hers in return.

"It's okay, Joshie," she had said reassuringly to her three-year old. The little blonde boy turned curious blue eyes to hers.

"Big flyer," said Josh. He was describing the baby great falcon, almost his height, which stood on the living room rug with him. In preparation for this day they had protected him as best they could from thinking of the birds as natural enemies or of himself as their natural prey. They knew in their marrow the only hope for peace in their world lay in connections like the one they were trying to build between their son Josh and the young Cor. Nonetheless, they felt terrified.

The baby bird wasn't paying much attention to Josh. Cor cocked his head and curled his talons to feel the unaccustomed rug, ripping the material. A sound came from his mother, Rab, watching from the other side of the room. She, too, was afraid. "Sorry," she said softly.

Her husband Cam beside her tried to catch the humans' eyes. If this didn't work, he would lose all credibility in his clan and be forever beyond the feeding circle. His piercing raptor gaze met the human mother's.

"It's all right, isn't it?" Cam asked. Audra could only nod, but now her husband spoke.

"Sure it is. Hey, Josh, this is Cor. He's Aunt Rab and Uncle Cam's little boy." He blushed. Jeb hadn't planned to call the young bird a boy, but the other names that came to mind were all unfriendly. Cam lowered his lids and cocked his head reassuringly in what the humans had come to recognize as a smile.

"That's right," he said. "Cor, you see this nestling, Josh?" Cor fixed Josh with a stare and finally shrieked, making both mothers jump, even though the noise was like a laugh.

"No feathers!" Cor announced. Jeb spoke again. "Just like us, Cor. You know us. We've been in your feeding circle." Cor looked at Jeb and back to Josh.

Now Cam took over. "We thought it was time for the two of you to meet. We want you to be friends." Josh took a long look at Cor's dad, as if wondering whether he really meant it. Then he took the few steps over to Cor and threw an arm around him.

Cor looked at the hand dangling over his shoulder and shriek-laughed again. Josh's mother turned away and grabbed her husband's arm with both hands to keep from snatching Josh to safety. With her back turned she heard Josh say "Soft" and Cor say "Warm." Then Josh gave a human laugh and Cor tried to imitate him and Audra burst into tears.

That had been seventeen years ago, but the memory had all the vividness of terror. She turned to her best friend, standing patiently by. "Oh, Rab, I was so frightened."

Rab spread a comforting wing over her shoulders and cooed soothingly, "I know, I know…Me, too." All of a sudden Audra realized that part of her bond with this falcon had been their mother-fear, that they were risking their sons' lives, she literally and Rab by chancing Cor's place in the feeding circle, with the inevitably shortened life that followed expulsion. She hugged Rab close and they leaned their heads together.

"Mom, say, Mom!" The now-grown Josh burst into the room. "Hey, Aunt Rab. What's wrong?"

"I'm sorry, Joshie." Audra hadn't called him that in years. "I was remembering when we introduced you to Cor. Not even having your father travel in the war zone scared me as much as that did."

Josh just grinned, not from carelessness – it bothered him to think of his beloved Mom so frightened – but out of sheer vitality and high spirits. "But now you're really glad at how it worked out, right?"

"Oh, yes. Really glad." She stroked his light hair tenderly, still seeing the child and boy in this handsome young man with his oddly piercing blue eyes. She wondered if putting intelligent species so close together made them more alike in subtle ways. As if in answer she heard Cor's human-sounding chuckle before he entered the room. The full-grown grand falcon was a head taller than Josh, who was already tall for a human, but she always thought of Cor as little, probably, she now realized, to minimize any residual fear.

"Cor, sweetie! Come get a preen." The huge bird tucked his head gently into her shoulder and she smoothed his neck and shoulder feathers.

Rab spoke up. "Now, when do you two have air space?"

Josh exclaimed, "That's what I came to tell you. We're going now and the Council will be watching to see if they like us."

"They will," Cor's confidence made him seem even bigger, if possible.

Rab and Audra secretly agreed, but they held themselves in check, always showing control, as they had had to in building this community. Audra hugged her friend close and spoke for them both. "You know how excited we'll be if you get to go to the games. Now, let's go."

They walked out of the living room onto the balcony, a rock projection like hundreds of others jutting out from the sides of a huge, luminous cavern. Grand falcons flew everywhere. Some carried humans below them on perches. To let them dismount the birds braked just above a balcony and the humans hopped down and turned immediately to grab and fold the perch mechanisms into compact cylinders.

Cor and Josh looked up toward the Council Chamber, a space with an unusually broad ledge holding five falcons and five humans. "They're almost assembled," Josh noted. "I hope Dad and Uncle Cam are already there. Time to call for space."

Cor needed little encouragement. He stretched, fluffed his feathers out and gave the wild shriek that claimed the air. Josh and his mother took their hands from their ears and the four of them watched as all the flyers came slowly to rest. Finally only one pair remained, Cor's father carrying Josh's to the chamber. Cor raised a wing a bit awkwardly and pointed with the small, weak four-fingered hand at the end of it. "Look," he said. "They can't vote on this, can they?"

"I don't think so," Josh answered. "But you know them. They have to go be visibly immovable to show what strong stock we come from." Cor chuckled and Rab and Audra nearly laughed, too, surprised by the accurate account. Josh checked the thick leathers on his wrists while Cor watched.

They looked around. The air was clear. Every balcony was full – adults, children, nestlings, groundlings, everyone who could was watching. The two friends stood at the edge of their stone ledge hundreds of feet in the air and Cor muttered, "Ready, steady, dive!"

Both of them pushed outward, Josh twisting and flipping in the air, Cor plummeting nearby in a tight-winged spiral around him. Suddenly Cor reached out with his talons, grabbed Josh by the wrists and started to fly upward.

They repeated that sequence three times at different heights and with increasingly difficult tumbling by Josh and Cor. Sometimes Josh held Cor's legs and flipped, releasing and catching him, or held positions like a dancer below him. Twice Cor dove and pulled up to flip Josh high above him only to catch him in mid-spin as he fell past.

Finally Cor threw Josh precisely up and over toward a deep empty ledge, so that he landed as lightly as if he had stepped off a stool onto it. The falcon flew further up as Josh stood in triumph, arms raised.

A smattering of appreciative noise began. Right in front of the Council Cor gathered himself and fell, as if toward prey, right for the unprotected Josh. Despite the years of peace inside the cavern, many held their breaths, afraid that something had gone horribly wrong and that the falcon would kill the trusting human before their eyes.

At the last possible moment Cor's wings opened to stall him and he flipped over to rest folded tight on his back on Josh's hands. The human bent his arms and knelt on one knee to keep his balance as he held the huge bird aloft. Though the falcon's bones were mostly air, he was still heavy. Josh rose and heaved the sleek body up to spin in the air and be caught again.

Now the watching falcons gasped: to let the human break his fall without opening his wings! Such trust. Again and again Josh tossed Cor and caught him, till finally he let his arms fall at his sides and Cor opened his wings to drift down behind him. The cavern exploded with noise as all the falcons shrieked their joy. The humans had to cover their ears, but they, too, yelled and whistled and stomped.

In the Council chamber the leaders of Cavernhome gathered, but none made for the seats and perches around the Council table. They were too excited, though none said a word. Josh's father and Cam stood stiffly, not looking at each other, while colleagues of both species rustled around them.

The youngest falcon broke the silence. "Aiyee! A triumph." Suddenly everyone was talking and the two proud parents were grinning and looking at each other in amazement.

"Breathtaking."

"Unbelievably original."

"It's as if they made peace into a dance."

"And trust."

"So skilled."

"They are the embodiment of all we stand for."

"Complete mastery of their strengths."

"Complete interdependence."

"They must go to the commensal games on behalf of this planet."

"Let us discuss that very point. Ladies and gentlemen?" The speaker, the only falcon older than Cam, gestured with one hand toward the table and everyone sat or perched around it, as quickly solemn as they had been exuberant a moment before. It would not be so simple to send Josh and Cor to the games. The cost would be huge. Then, to reach the neutral port city they would have to travel through the war zone.

III

Tock And Tom

In another council on another planet, the leader sighed with frustration. Plish Coldsea was a handsome green woman with darker green hair and big expressive brown eyes in a smoothly impassive face. She pinched her nostrils shut to express her impatience and spread her toes beneath the water so that her webbing could create a satisfying current when she jiggled her foot. Several of the dolphin representatives around the stone slab table took this opportunity to slip off into the water to rewet their heads. They made sure to keep their expressive features still, but Plish could just imagine their exaggerated expressions of annoyance out of sight of the assemblage. The green people, who required less immersion, stayed seated.

Plish tried again, "I know eleven generations seems very far away, Tom, but we really do need to act now." The strong young man sitting across from her nodded assent and his curly green hair flopped briefly in his face, so that he tossed it back gracefully. He didn't mean to disagree with anyone, but he really didn't see how he could do this job the Assembly was trying to assign to him.

"Okay, okay." Tom gestured amiably around the table. "Hey, better heads than mine, right? But that's just it, ma'am, you could do better than me and Tock. No offense, poddy," he turned with sudden concern to his dolphin pal by his side. Tom would sooner take on a sea snake barehanded that hurt Tock's feelings. That depth of caring and loyalty overwhelmed Tock every time he experienced it.

"Fret not, fish-boy," Tock teased him back. "They could certainly do better than us."

In fact, Tock had done brilliantly at his studies, despite having the much slower Tom assigned him as lab partner to provide hands. Tock could probably understand all the math, astronomy and biology that had gone into the Planet Science Directorate's finding. But that had not been the Assembly's reason for choosing this inseparable pair, who called themselves the lagoon goons and acted like it much of the time.

The oldest dolphin, Dom of Southsea spoke to Tock directly, using their ancient riddling technique to help him discover the truth. "What must the team we send be able to do first?" he began. Tock recognized Dom's approach and thought carefully before answering.

"The team you send. I guess they have to swim well enough to qualify for these games you talk about where all the planets will be represented." He and Tom made it on that count anyway.

"Yes." Dom glowered at Tom, who stopped sloshing his hand back and forth and tried to look serious but only managed to look friendly. "You must qualify for the games. And once you are there, what qualities might be useful in establishing the kinds of connections we seek?" Tom's friendliness began to look a little vacant. He hoped Tock would keep answering, because he had no clue himself.

Tock resorted to thinking out loud, watching Dom intently for signs of agreement or disapproval. "Well, we want connections…to lots of different sorts of peoples…not just water people, but other sorts…and for that, I guess, geniality would be useful…maybe adaptability…being, well, likable." Dom nodded vigorously.

"Us?" Tom asked.

"Yeah, " Tock answered. "They don't think we have to understand anything. We just have to be so cute somebody wants to adopt us." Dom looked exasperated, but Plish actually giggled. In her view Tock had just summarized the Assembly's long debate leading up to the choice of Tock and Tom as envoys to the games.

The dolphin nearest Dom glared at Plish and continued, "We do think understanding will matter. We want you to be able to make the threat to our planet believable."

"That part'll be up to you, Tock," said Tom. He was beginning to accept there was no way out of this. Better just make the best of it.

Tock made a face, as if he were going to object, but all he said was, "You'll convince 'em, too, poddy. You think it's a real problem, right?"

"Heating up? You know it. I hate it too warm. And the Leader said only eleven generations left to go. I wonder what it'll be like here after we leave." Despite his slow thinking Tom did have the adaptability Tock had mentioned. He had fully accepted the discovery that their sun had begun expansion and would boil them alive if they didn't find a new planet. His musing brought a thoughtful quiet to the group.

Tom himself broke the silence. "When we find a place where they want us, how will we get there?"

This produced a visible, though unvocalized split within the Assembly, with some of both dolphins and green people squirming or making faces, while the rested affected to be totally unconcerned. Plish decided someone official and important could voice the answer, as unsatisfying as it might be.

"I call on Kip of Deepsea as Leader of the Science Directorate." Everyone grew still and concentrated on a smallish dolphin off to one side. Though atechnological, both species depended heavily on the Directorate to tell them when and where to fish to keep the planet healthy. The massed attention of the dolphins was almost palpable. The less intellectual green people added their own quality to the waiting silence, something close to tenderness.

Kip spoke simply. "We do not know with certainty that there is a way to transport whole populations from planet to planet. Already our birth rates are dropping. There will be fewer of us with each succeeding generation. And the intergalactic games are giving the interplanetary authority a chance to move many species over vast distances. We hope that a new home will be found, because it must be. We hope that a way to move us all will be found, because it must be. We will pay the authority to move you two to the games by allowing them to mine the large landmass between Southsea and Northsea. Perhaps they will find something so valuable to them that we can pay to move everyone in time. We have no certain answers, but we face a certain doom, so we must do what we can. You must do what you can."

The gravity of her speech weighed on everyone, even the irrepressible Tom. But he finally recovered and gave them all a green version of a grin. "I can do that much, especially since it involves swimming!" And he leapt up from the rock he'd been sitting on, started a lovely dive, then turned it into a splashing flop at the last moment. The Assembly groaned at this childish joke, but they whistled and clapped, too, as if they were watching wavedancers. Tock slipped away to join him and tossed Tom in the air, once and again higher, then followed him with a leap of his own in breathtaking unison. They played and played, with Tom seeming to tumble on the very surface of the water, using the surging Tock as his base for leaps and landings, then with both of them airborn again for a final series of twisting, spinning dives.

IV

Amanda And David

AMANDA WANTED David to stop grazing and take her down to the river for a swim. "Pleease!" she called to the horse from the protective shade of the maple tree. David whiffled softly to let her know he was considering her request and after a couple more mouthfuls of the alfalfa he meandered toward her.

"You humans do not tolerate cold and heat very well," he thought.

"I know, I know," answered Amanda, who read him perfectly, but hadn't quite mastered the art of thinking her reply back to him. "We're a puny species, notable only for opposable thumbs, insistent vocalizations and the inability to let things be."

David whuffled again, coming as close as he ever did to laughing out loud. He was so fond of this little brown scampery person who understood him so well.

He must have thought some of that out loud, because Amanda answered, "Didn't anyone, I mean any human, ever understand you before me?'

"Not so well. Your mother felt the moods of all my people, and her father is said to have been like you…nosy." He turned his head to the side where she was standing playing with his mane, and pushed her backward with his own big dark brown nose.

"Hey!" she protested. "No fair just because you're bigger than I am. River?"

"River," he answered, aware that he'd enjoy a drink and the chance to stand and cool his legs in the fresh running water.

Amanda jumped up to sit on David's back and squeezed with her legs, not because he needed that kind of old-fashioned communication, but simply from instinct distilled over all the generations her people had worked with horses. As David wheeled and loped across the meadow she felt her usual gratitude and joy that she had been able to grow up out here in one of the last sparsely populated areas of earth. Had she been around other people, she might never have learned to listen so well to the voices in her mind that turned out to belong to the horses on her family's ranch.

"I have thought something similar," David said. Amanda realized that she must have thought 'out loud.' "My people have grown better at speaking and listening over the years, and yours may also be improving, but you may have trouble hearing with your minds if you listen to each other with your ears too much."

At the river David sped down the bank and galloped headlong into the swimming hole at the bend in the waterway. Halfway in he stopped hard, lowering his head and Amanda tumbled forward into the water, squealing and laughing. She swam against the current, giving herself a good workout even while she cooled off. David waded upstream a bit to drink where the sand hadn't been stirred up, but he stayed aware of her constantly, as she did him.

When her mother was still alive, Amanda had once explained to her and Grandpa that she and David were "In the same family. It doesn't matter that he's not a human being. He's a person, just like us and he's family." In her mother and her grandfather the blood of the plains tribes ran strong, and this made sense to them.

Her much older half brother, Asa, had no understanding of it at all, but he was accustomed to the planets with multiple intelligent species from his work in galactic diplomacy, so he kept his mouth shut in front of Amanda. Just the same she thought of him as one of "them," the people who considered humans earth's only intelligent species. She had run away from him as soon as she could after their mother died. Asa had looked for her for weeks. And though they had never known their fathers, she was completely unmoved by Asa's final desperate plea – "We're the only family we've got." When he saw her hardness, he had turned cold himself. "Fine, then. Live out here away from everything. I don't care what happens to you." That had given her just a moment of hesitation, but she had decided quickly that he didn't really mean it, and she had been completely content with her decision.

Amanda splashed out of the water and stood dripping happily on the shore. The time had come, she thought, and felt no surprise this time when David heard her.

"Are you sure we need to do this?" He asked. They both dreaded riding into the port city with its paving, crowds, traffic and noise and the artificial smell of conditioned air.

"Yes. You agree with me. You know you do. We have to show them what is possible."

"And this will result in a wholesale transformation of attitudes," David said wryly.

"Well, maybe not. Probably no. But we have to give them the chance," she concluded. After all, people might be ready to learn, even it they were too slow to change themselves and too fast to change whatever they could get their hands on.

David plunged into the river before coming out, then shook like a dog before Amanda climbed back on him. The day's heat dried them before they were halfway to the port, so they chose the meandering route of the underground stream, longer than the road, but somewhat treed, shady and private.

Half a mile from the huge bubble of the port city they stopped under ancient cottonwoods. "Thirsty trees," David said. "I can smell the water."

Amanda ran her fingers trough her long tan hair. "Look, David." She held out the strands she was braiding. "The sun's made it lighter, so it's the same color as you."

David wondered if his dark mane and tail matched the deeper brown of her skin, as if he could magically have a human daughter. Though she hadn't heard this private thought, Amanda answered, "And my hand is the same as your mane. Grandpa used to say we are all children of the stars, made from the light of wisdom, trying to return to that light. Maybe you're my brother or something." David snorted to put an end to this foolishness, then trotted a few steps away. She needed to walk a bit to stay limber if they were going to ride for her real brother, the Ambassador.

Amanda picked her way among the trees and underbrush, looking as aimless as a butterfly, but actually heading for what she considered the most important spot on the earth. David followed a few paces behind. Amanda pressed around the last thicket and emerged into the shady glen where her mother was buried. The season had been so hot that the small pool at the far end was nearly choked with reeds, but as always the place was awash in birdsong. The aspens on the south side fluttered grey-green even on this airless day, dappling the sun that made it through the leaves.

She walked over to the granite headstone and read "Felicity Bramble". They had thought about having it read "Happy," since everybody called her that. They hadn't been able to find out when she was born to put dates on it, but in the end they settled for her real name and a second line "Beloved Mother". Amanda placed the river pebble she had been carrying in the collection atop the stone, one for every year since her mother had died. She stared at the pebbles and slowly realized what she was seeing. There were too many, at least a handful. Someone else had been here, too. It must have been Asa, Amanda thought. She had just never noticed before. She had never needed anything from him before either, she admitted. This was a handy time, she mused wryly, to think they had something in common.

"David," she called softly. "Come see." He ambled over and looked at the gravestone.

"I see," he acknowledged. They stood together for a while, feeling the serenity of the place, listening to the birds, enjoying their memories.

That turned out to be their last peaceful moment together for some time to come. First Amanda dealt with the three skeptical port entry officials about her lack of electronic identification and her plan to see her brother without an appointment. Finally they found her fingerprint record, held a strained conversation with her brother's office about her refusal of an official ride across town, and let them go. David had begun to jig about restlessly by the time she had worked out their route through the city's parks to government headquarters.

"What's the matter with you? Calm down!" Her command actually helped him, but David stayed tense. "Is it all the people?" Amanda asked. "I mean, can you hear them thinking?"

"No!" David replied brusquely. "Humans are very unclear. Very unclear. I understand very little. Except you."

"But you know what they're saying," she said.

"No!" he insisted again. "All that nonsense at the entrance was just mud, mud. You are the only clear human I know." Amanda felt baffled, but she knew enough to take his word for it. She had simply never thought to talk to him about it before. For a second she had a terrible sinking doubt about her whole campaign. Then she rallied. She took control as best she could to give him something to concentrate on and David was grateful. It took them three tries to get into the elevator in her brother's building, because David wouldn't go in with other people. He was sweating lightly by the time she hauled her brother into the auditorium to watch them.

"You want me to believe that this horse communicates with you just as I do, but I'm telling you, we don't need to have that fight again. I've had advice on the matter and earth will send you to the games and let them decide there if you qualify." The tall, thin man looked down at her from what seemed an enormous distance.

"You don't even want to watch what we can do, do you?" Amanda accused him. "You just want to send us away." On the stage across the room David heard Asa's thought as distinctly as if it had come from Amanda. It was a cry of anguish. "I miss her so much." Then nothing more, just the usual buzz of conflicted static humans put out all the time. David knew he must mean their mother, whom Amanda resembled more by the day. Before she could say even angrier words, David spoke to her.

"Control yourself. He's doing the best he can." Amanda made a visible effort. Her brother seemed to catch himself as well and responded to her accusation.

"No, no, Amanda. Of course I want to see you. In fact I want to show you off. Give us fifteen minutes for a call to go out, so whoever's free can come see you, too."

So it was that Amanda and David waited unhappily back stage as an excited audience began to gather. "This will be good practice," David said.

"I know," she replied. "I just can't believe how disappointed I am not to be fighting with my brother. You'd think it would be a relief, but I feel so cheated."

“I know. Try to concentrate. It helps me.” David admonished.

“I will. I wonder when we’ll be going to the games.” Her brother had stepped into the wings in time to hear her remarks, and though he couldn’t hear David, he realized they must have been talking to each other.

“You can go right after this.” Amanda and David both looked astonished, but neither objected, so he finally asked, “Shall I introduce you?”

V

The New World

JULA AWOKE looking into the warm blue eyes of a young man staring right back at her. She knew she ought to introduce herself, but all she could say was, "Yours are green." And after an unblinking pause that seemed to last forever, he said, "Yes."

He was dark-haired like her, not much taller than she, but maybe older, she guessed. He wore his swarm of iridescent green butterflies like clothing, just as she did, but his moved around more. She thought that might be what made him seem restless.

"Are you with the Grounders?" She asked, though she knew the answer. Yesterday she'd fled as far as she could into the jungle and had fallen asleep on a mossy cliff top overlooking a river valley she had never seen before. This far from the five small settlements, he must be one of the Grounders.

"I'm their leader," he answered. They both seemed mesmerized by the other. Neither had ever imagined finding another person with a swarm.

"Are you Hank Wilson?" Jula named the first one to have left a settlement, long before anyone realized it was a trend. Settlers mentioned him to this day, because his alarmed father still lead efforts to infiltrate the jungle and trap the children who had disappeared. He frowned briefly and his greens shifted in a way Jula could read as discomfort.

"Yes," he acknowledged. "Just Hank." He had gone to ground years ago and had never been spotted since. He seemed healthy enough, she thought, inspecting his greens for the telltale dullness or damage that would reveal any problems in his body. He seemed strong and friendly, easy to imagine as someone others could trust, yet there was something unhappy about him too.

"How many are with you?"

"Around forty," he answered. "Everybody's always coming and going." Forty! More than she had realized. All the settlements must be involved.

"Do you go back to visit?" Jula asked.

"Not me." Hank stood up and looked over the valley. His greens rearranged themselves, but didn't settle fully. "It's dangerous. Even if they don't go inside or anything. There could be an ambush in somebody's back yard."

"But nobody's ever been caught, have they?"

"No," he conceded with a grin. "Come on. I'll introduce you to everybody else. What's your name?"

"Jula," she said, and suddenly felt shy. Her blues formed a high collar, long sleeves and long skirt, leaving only her head and hands uncovered.

They walked for a couple of hours through the jungle on the slope going down into the valley. The vegetation looked impenetrable, and would have been for anyone trying blindly to forge straight ahead. Hank read the drape of vines and the density of branches so well, that they never once had to stop and redirect their way. Zigging and zagging with every step they moved steadily ahead. Jula realized even the savviest in jungle trekking from her settlement would have used a machete sometimes, but they never even broke a branch. Mostly they went in silence, enjoying the bird song, the frog calls, the click and whirr of insects all around.

At a resting point Jula thought to ask, "How did you find me?"

"My greens," Hank answered without hesitation. "They let me know whenever there's someone new. With you they just…seemed to know more, like exactly where you were." Jula wondered if her blues were in contact with his greens and got a happy affirmative in response.

The walk gave her time to think through what she wanted to do. Yesterday's flight had satisfied her deep need to be away, away from her mother and father, away from the concentration of human-made houses and things, away from pavement and carpet and flooring that kept her feet off the welcoming earth. Now that she felt free of all she didn't want, she checked to see if she still did want to dance and go to the games. Her answer and the blues' was a big, excited yes. When they entered the encampment at the base of the hill, she had no idea what an impression of strength and purpose she and Hank made.

At first she thought it was just a clearing formed by a circle of elnut trees, with a few young people sitting on stones and talking in the middle. Gradually she realized there were hammocks strung from trunk to trunk and nests in the branches of the trees. And many of these held people. A tall boy with a big-eyed bird on one shoulder rose to greet them. He said what they always said to each other, even if they had only been gone a brief while. "Welcome home." And then, "Who's the new one?"

"Jula Mirova," she answered. Hank shook his head and said, "Just Jula now." And though she felt so right out here far from sight or sound of any settlement, she didn't like giving up her family name. "I don't know about that," she thought to herself, and to her surprise her blues nestled in close as they did when they liked how she felt.

She had no time to wonder about that, because everyone streamed over for introductions. All had companions – mammals, birds, a few insects, reptiles – they never separated from. Each person stepped up and said, "Welcome home," gave a name, then explained, "This is my riverdog," or "This is my twigsinger," and so forth. None of the companions had a name, a fact Jula had never noticed till now.

In response to each one she said, "Jula. My blues," till the clearing was full and everyone had spoken. Then they waited, in silence, as if they expected more from her. "Thank you," she offered. Still they waited. "I'm glad to be…home," she finally said, and this turned out to be the right phrase, releasing everyone to chatter and relax.

A girl almost her age named Maggie showed Jula how to hollow out a cakefuit. "We'll have the juicy part for supper," she explained. "And you keep the shell for your things. Oh, that's right, you didn't bring anything. Never mind, you may bring stuff back from a visit some time."

The others' 'stuff' turned out to be clothing, books, art supplies, writing materials, musical instruments, almost anything that required no technology. "You don't have communicators," Jula realized. "How do you manage?"

For explanation Maggie turned to the white warbler perched on her shoulder and said, "Say hi-to-Bobbie, hi-to-Bobbie." The bird stretched its neck gracefully and gave a high-pitched multi-note call almost immediately repeated at a distance in the jungle. "Bobbie's my twin," Maggie explained. "She's off on a mapping expedition. It turns out these birds are fantastic imitators, so we devised a simple substitution code and we use them like an ancient telegraph."

Jula heard the jungle bird call again, differently this time, and then Maggie's white repeated the new series of notes. "Bobbie says hi back. They're seven days out, farther than we've ever been before." She went off to tell the others this proud news, and Jula mulled over what she'd just seen.

"Professor," she called over to the boy she had first met. "How do you keep your field notes? Without a communicator to store them?"

Professor looked up from his notebook and then held it and his pencil out to demonstrate. "Old-fashioned. Once in a while I go back and data dump where I came from. They like our work back there. I've discovered lots of interactive plant systems, for example. And many more edibles than they use. Everything except altricial species. We seem to be the only one of those on the planet."

"Dr. Gould would love you." Jula named the planet's chief biologist, one settlement over from hers.

Professor grinned. "He does. That's my dad." Jula just laughed out loud. Most Grounders seemed completely comfortable with having left their families to 'come home.' And many talked as if their families were at peace with it, too, contrary to the way it had been discussed around her dinner table back in the settlement.

Jula fell asleep that night in a hammock of grass-rope, her mind swirling with new friends, new sights and smells, and new ideas. Her last surprised, happy thought was that she really did feel at home here.

On the other hand, Jula realized the next morning she thought some of the Grounders were just too young to be on their own. She and Hank were among the oldest, of course, since they had been among the first born on this world. She saw that the youngest tended to cluster around him, even if they were playing among themselves, and he often had kids sitting close by, someone asking him to settle a tiff, maybe even someone leaning against him or getting a comforting hug.

Before long Jula had her own cluster, kids seven years younger or more. One of them fell from a hammock being swung too hard, scraped a palm slightly and came crying to her.

"Let me see," she was business-like but completely reassuring at the same time, much like her own parents, whom she suddenly missed. The injury was a lot smaller than the fuss being made over it. Jula hugged the little boy and asked, "You miss your mom, don't you?" He just nodded his head against her. "Do you go back to visit?"

The crying stopped abruptly. "Hank doesn't want us to. He's afraid they'll try to keep us." Jula scowled at what seemed like meanness to her.

"What do you think?" She asked.

"I think Mom misses me and if I asked her to she'd let me come back home."

"Do you know how to get back where you came from, Evan?"

He grinned and pointed. "Two days from here."

"Are you okay to go by yourself? Just you and your huggy?" She patted the furry creature hanging around Evan's neck using one soft paw to stroke the boy's hair.

"I don't have to go alone. Lucy and Kyle want to go back to visit, too."

"Well, then," Jula said, as if all were settled. "Hank told me everyone comes and goes when they want."

"We'll be back home in a few days," said the now beaming Evan. He ran off happily and Jula realized that Hank had been watching.

"Some of these kids are too little to be on their own," she accused.

"They're fine. You can see for yourself they're healthy," Hank defended. "And they're obviously not alone."

"But they need their families." She insisted.

Hank's face darkened and he turned away. "I never tell anybody they have to stay," he sounded miserable.

"But when they're that little, they figure out what you want and do it anyway." She accused. "What are you so afraid of back there, anyway? Were you in trouble? Is that why you ran away?"

Hank shrank in on himself. "I don't talk about it," he offered finally. His voice sounded deep and cloudy, as if it had been pushed down in him.

"But you can talk to me," Jula said, realizing as she said it that Hank had looked at her in that funny way ever since she arrived because he trusted her.

They walked together out of the grove. After a while Hank sat on the ground and started to talk. "Once I was out in the jungle I knew I was home. All the settlement people still wore shoes back then, and I remember taking mine off and how I felt…so glad…so safe. My parents…I think there's something wrong with my dad and my mother was afraid." He stalled out, so Jula tried to help.

"Did he hurt you?"

"No. Not yet. But the older I got the more it looked like he would. He didn't do that much. It's just…he hated me."

Jula tried to imagine and realized she couldn't. "What did that do to you?" Hank stared at her thoughtfully and the pause grew long. Somehow she knew if she gave him time, he would be able to tell her more.

"You see my greens." Hank spread his arms and the greens covered them and him and flowed out onto the ground around him like a beautiful cloth.

"They're beautiful," Jula acknowledged.

"When I went to ground, they barely covered my shoulders." Jula started in astonishment. She hadn't had so few since she was tiny. "I'm not sure, of course," he continued. "But I think being safe makes me healthier, and that makes them healthier." Jula nodded. "When I saw you, and your blues I thought, somebody must love her very much." Jula smiled and nodded again.

"Do you miss your family? The rest of them?" She asked.

"Not really…except...My mother wanted me to go. She's…," he struggled against his loyalty to say more about her and how glad she had seemed to have him out of her world. Finally he just shrugged his shoulders. "I have a baby brother." His voice caught and he couldn't talk.

"And you've never been back to check on him."

Hank turned to her with tears in his eyes. "Nobody who's gone to ground since early on can tell me anything about him. And he's older now. Not anywhere near as old as I was then, and he does have a riverdog that would protect him, but I keep wondering."

"And what keeps you from going back to check?" she asked. His greens swirled out in confused eddies and he didn't have to say anything. "It's not safe for you. Your greens know."

He nodded miserably. "They tell me to stay home. They want me to help the little ones here." Jula reached out to touch his hand.

"They would never tell you something that wasn't good for you, would they?"

"No, never." He smiled a little as if this did comfort him. "I just worry. And I envy the ones who go back to visit. And sometimes it's a little hard to tell whether my greens think something would be good for me or good for everybody."

Jula laughed, recognizing the problem. "It's as if they have a hard time saying anything personal. It's more like good-for-the-planet, bad-for-the-planet, just like my father." Suddenly she felt bashful, and stopped talking. But she didn't regret giving trust for trust.

Hank managed a small smile. "Thank you for listening. I do feel better now."

Jula thought a bit. "Maybe you have family here, at home. People who have become family to you? You've been out how long? Five years?"

Now Hank seemed less comfortable again. "I never thought about that. I guess most of the kids seem to need me to be kind of a big brother. But I don't think it's like real family, do you?" He made 'real family' sound like something bad.

"I don't know. Maybe where you feel at home you can make a family. Five years is a long time," she said softly.

His voice thickened again. "You're the first one I've told about my....the people I came from. They miss theirs. It seemed mean to tell them I was so glad to be away. You miss yours, too, but I didn't think you'd mind." Jula remembered how accusing she had felt of him earlier.

"Oh, no, not at all. I want you to trust me. I feel..." She didn't know how to name what she felt. "We should be friends." She had almost said they should be together, the way you might to a boyfriend. But she didn't think about boys that way. She got up and turned back toward the grove and he seemed to accept this as fitting. "Have you heard me talking about the intergalactic games?"

"A little," he answered. "It sounds as if you want to leave me as soon as you've met me, friend." He was just teasing, but she stared at him hard a moment to see if he might be thinking about her in that other way.

"If I could figure out how to get to the port in time, I would."

"Oh, we can get you there," he said.

"You're kidding! How? You? You have no technology!"

"Calm down," he laughed. "We'll have a thinkout at dinner tonight and get it all set." With that he strode ahead of her back toward the grove. And she found, as she had walking with him the day before, that she could hardly keep up, let alone talk the while.

VI

Facing War

COR COULDN'T keep up with the grand falcon training them as they ran among the boulders. He consoled himself that Josh could barely keep up, too, even with his much longer stride. The Sergeant made the command sign to stop and the two of them leaned exhausted against a large rock. Cor and Josh both hated being away from Cavernhome, but their purpose demanded that they train on the planet's surface, closer to danger every day.

"I've never seen you winded," Josh huffed in a whisper. The sweat ran down his face, making dirty streaks through the dust that coated everything.

"I'm not much good at pretending to be at war," Cor managed between heaving breaths.

A noise like rock hitting rock sounded close by and the boulder beside Josh's shoulder suddenly chipped. A fragment hit him in the face and a trickle of blood erupted.

Josh said, "Ow!" and put his hand up just as the Sergeant fell to the earth and signaled them to follow.

"What happened?" Cor asked.

"Shot," the tough old raptor answered. At the same time Josh and Cor realized the Sergeant was bleeding, soaking his breast plumage. Josh reached out a hand to find the wound and help him up. The Sergeant's powerful beak lunged out and snapped by Josh's hand. "Don't touch me," the Sergeant ordered. "They might be watching. Training's over. You're on your own. Go."

"No," said Cor. "We won't leave you." He raised one wing to shield the Sergeant, turned and fired back in the direction of the attack with the heat seeker attached to his hand at the end of the other wing.

"Disengage," the sergeant ordered, and despite the brevity of their training, Cor obeyed.

"If we leave you here, you'll die," Josh argued. "You've only just come to us. You have a life of peace ahead of you."

The Sergeant interrupted by grabbing his ankle with one foot. "I have a lifetime of war behind me." He sounded so tired he might be a thousand years old. "I defected just when you needed me. Now remember your lessons. Neither side wants you to make it to those games."

"We don't have all our equipment," Cor protested.

"If you go back to Cavernhome now, you'll lead these attackers right to it." They all knew what that meant. Wherever peace cells had been discovered on the planet's surface, everyone had been massacred. By either side. Cavernhome was the largest combined community they had and the only one where the young of both species could grow up in relative safety. "Head for the port. Now. Steal transport if you can."

Josh and Cor looked at each other. "That's an order," the Sergeant was weakening, but his voice still commanded. They turned to him and said, "Yes, sir!" like the raw troops they were. Josh saluted as if the Sergeant were a human, held his weapon close, checked ahead and ran crouching. Cor followed closely.

They heard the telltale whistle of a heatseeker and realized that the Sergeant had somehow managed to fire. Then they heard the clatter human weapons made. Then silence.

Days later they trudged along a path through stony hills, Josh in the lead, Cor behind with fettered legs and a grim-looking collar chained slackly from his neck to Josh's wrist like a leash.

"Vole," Cor said softly. They stopped in their tracks.

"Where?" Josh asked.

"Two o'clock, one span out."

"Got it." Nothing moved but their eyes as they followed the little herbivore among the low plants.

"I'm starving," said Josh.

"Here comes dinner," answered Cor, as he ducked his head, shedding the collar, took one wing beat into the air and fell faster than a rock on the scurrying creature. He would have held its carcass high with one foot but his shackles didn't let him.

Josh sped over. "This is great! We can cook it as soon as it's dark." Cor stiffened and pointed with one talon to the hillside behind Josh.

"Well, lookee here!" Josh spun to see who belonged to the voice. Three humans in the same desert camouflage he wore were walking warily toward him. They looked half-starved, filthy and maybe injured.

"Stop there," Josh tried to take command as he had been taught. The peoples of Cavernhome were taller and bigger than any of the warriors except officers. "Identify yourselves." The rough trio did stop, but they didn't look as if they took any orders they didn't want to.

Their spokesman, the toughest, took a good look at Cor. "What you got here, Captain? You turn a big ole falcon like this into a hand hawk? Hunt your supper for you?"

"Identify yourselves," Josh bellowed, raising his rifle to firing position.

"Jesser, Fielder, Squints," he pointed. Squints had apparently earned this name. "I forgot your real name, Squints. Tell the Captain."

Squints moved closer to Cor, as if to see him better and finally said, "Private Olney," then turned back to Jesser to observe, "I never seen one this big and he's not hurt or nothing. We could eat for a month off him."

Cor started to raise the feathers around his neck and shoulders, but stopped quickly. His only real defense at this point was his supposed captor Josh. "Hands off, you stupid grunt." Josh was amazed at how vicious he sounded with his friend under threat. "You've never seen any officer that important in your whole wasted life, not even a brown-shitter. He gets delivered as is. By me."

Jesser thought he understood the situation now. "Ah, that's my Captain. Rutting after a promotion. Bring in this prize and get yourself declared king. Well, we'll just help you guard your fluffy trophy here and take some of the credit ourselves."

Josh's weapon wavered slightly, as if he might point it at Jesser. Instead the two stared hatefully at each other, while Josh tried desperately to figure out how to get rid of them. Finally, he conceded. "You can walk point, fifty paces ahead. Look for a place to camp tonight."

"We should split up to cover your back, too," Jesser pushed.

"You should shut your beak and follow orders. If you want a share in this."

Jesser reluctantly turned down the trail and the other two followed mindlessly. Cor thought that if Jesser told them to, they'd kill Josh in an instant. They fought only for their stomachs and killed whatever got in the way of the next meal. He wondered if the war had dried up the hearts of the grand falcons in the same way.

As Squints passed he reached down to take the vole carcass from Cor's talons and Cor thought briefly of killing him with a quick slash of the throat. Instead he held onto the vole just a moment, so that Squints looked up at him in astonishment from close range. Cor fleered him hard and the grubby soldier skittered away, ducking to make himself small, but clutching the game in his unweaponed hand.

As the three walked ahead Cor's hearing picked up, "He's a mean one, Jesser. I don't like this." And Jesser's answering, "Shut up, bird brain. If this works, we eat longer than a month."

Josh helped Cor settle the collar as comfortably as possible, and when the three were out of earshot, said, "I couldn't think what else to do. We're only two days from the port. We'll get a chance to get away."

"Or to kill them," Cor added. He knew it would not be so easy for him to imagine killing falcons, but after a moment Josh agreed, "Or kill them."

Suddenly Cor broke for a moment, "Oh, Joshie," he cried softly, "If we ever make it, what will we have become?" Josh didn't even look at him, just gave the collar one last tug and walked ahead.

VII

Facing Death

Tom couldn't even look Tock in the face. He didn't think they were going to make it, but at least he'd die protecting his poddy. Tock floated helplessly on the surface, too paralyzed to swim, struggling for every breath. They had been swept by the biggest school of death floaters Tom had ever seen. All around them dolphins and fish bobbed stiffly, some already dead from the floaters' toxin, but too big for them to eat, others like Tock waiting helplessly for the flenshers that inevitably followed a school like this. Only the green people had immunity from the toxin, but since they were a favorite flensher food, they'd be as far away as possible.

Tom swam protectively by Tock's body. "Breathe, old fish. That's all you have to do. Just breathe. I'll get us out of this."

Tock concentrated as hard as he could on his lungs and heaved air into them. He was exhausted. He would have laughed, if he could, at the thought of Tom's rescuing him. Tock probably wouldn't even feel it when the flensher's jaws closed around him and it shook its huge sightless head to rip him into pieces it could swallow. But Tom would feel everything. Tock wanted desperately to shout at him, "Swim! Save yourself! Get out of here!" But no sound came out, only a little of the air he'd fought to breathe in and would fight just as hard to breathe out.

"Hey, matey! Get out of there. Swim in with us. Safety in numbers."

Tom raised himself vertically half out of the water to see where the voice came from. Green heads bobbed just beyond all the bodies in the light swell – six, ten, more. They must be on the surface hoping to remain undetected close by all the dead and dying. The speaker called again. "Come on. The flenshers can't be far away."

"I can't," Tom yelled. "My poddy, Tock, he's still alive. Help me get him out, will you?"

The greens chattered excitedly, yet even though it might doom them, they couldn't turn away from such a request. As they swam over, one said, "We'll pull him out where the current won't spread your smell, but we can't stay with you."

"How'd you get caught by the floaters?" Tom asked.

Another answered. "Scouting fish for the pod. You know how they clump up in front of floaters. We just thought we were the best scouts ever to find so many." Several laughed. Even the threat of flenshers couldn't keep green people from enjoying a joke.

They surrounded Tock and most went under water where they could swim best. Tom and another strong green stayed on the surface to pull Tock's rigid form by the flippers extended hard as boards at his sides. They began to move, the ones below pushing up as well as forward, so that Tock rose slightly. Tom's helper splashed water on Tock's exposed stomach, something Tom had forgotten to do in his anguish. "Thank you," he said feelingly.

They headed for where Tom had first spotted the greens and he realized that they were right about the currents. If they could somehow be motionless and unscented, the mindless rows of ripping fangs might pass them by.

Tom felt a little flicker of hope that brightened when he realized Tock was breathing better, still raggedly and hard, but more steadily. Beyond the edge of the poisoned creatures they ran into a mat of seaweed. It undulated with the swells, but it was thick enough to be impenetrable when they tried to part it, thick enough for a sea bird to stand on and call at them as if it wanted to scare them off.

"Matweed," Tom said grimly, as the green heads popped up all around. They were goners now. The green people would have to swim around the mat. That would be slow enough on the surface, much too slow lugging the paralyzed Tock.

Tock made a noise as they stopped swimming. "That's it. Keep breathing," Tom encouraged.

"We'll be going now," said one of the greens rather urgently. The other who had helped on the surface said, "I think he's trying to say something. 'Raaat' or something."

Indeed, Tock was staring as hard as he could at Tom and trying to make a sound with every tortured exhalation. "Ra…st….raa….ft."

"Raft!" Tom cried. "He's telling us to get up on the matweed and use it as a raft. You've heard the stories! C'mon!" He heaved at Tock as hard as he could and managed to get him about halfway on in a lopsided way. "Come on!" He yelled again. "There's plenty of room. If we stay still the flenchers won't find us."

The rest of the greens seemed skeptical. As much as the dolphins needed water on their skins, the greens needed to move. They were miserable holding still.

"I'd rather swim."

"We'd all rather swim."

"He's right, though. I had an uncle made it past a flensher stretched out on an old log. Said it came inches away, never even knew he was there."

That still might not have convinced everyone, but suddenly they all heard the thrash of flenshers tearing into the floater carrion at the far end of the zone of death. They scrambled, pushing and tugging at Tock, till they were all on the mat. Tock found that he breathed easier out of the water. The matweed was dense enough to hold them off the surface without breaking, though water seeped up in the depression made by each body.

"Remember, not a sound. No movement." Tom whispered the reminder. As they settled in they grew more aware of the grunts and splashes from the direction of the flenshers. There were four of them, and they crashed toward the matweed faster than anyone expected. Perhaps they had felt the vibrations of climbing onto the raft through their skin.

They had real hearing. Their huge pale eyeless heads betrayed their origin on the sea bottom, where no light could reach. Tock's people called them fangmouths because they seemed to be nothing but huge mouths full of teeth attached to stomachs. Their pale bodies seemed puny and atrophied in comparison to those big stupid heads with only nostrils to navigate with. Their fins were weak looking, split into scraggly tendrils, almost like stunted, useless hands and feet. They swam in jerky pulses without finesse. Almost anything could swim more agilely than a flensher, but they never tired, and even the youngest green people had nightmares of evading lunge after lunge after lunge of those vicious teeth with the jaws cracking shut closer and closer each time. Now, as they willed themselves to immobility, the green people and the dolphin heard death come toward them.

It was easiest for Tom. Tock couldn't move and Tom's loving loyalty banished any real urge to stir, despite the aching that filled every unused muscles. He would die or live with his poddy.

The other greens were in agony. Not moving was a torture for them. They threatened the young with it if they misbehaved. Now they listened helplessly as death approached, and they began to fear their pounding hearts and quivering guts would somehow give them away.

All mouths pressed grimly, tightly shut. All fear-wide eyes moved with the splashing of the frenzy. They could tell there were four flenshers and they could tell just about where they were. But it stunned them when they heard one of the heads thrashing from side to side to tear out a bite so close that the waves moved their mat. Then fish guts sprayed through the air and rained down on them as the prey fell apart.

The flensher grunted as it crunched the bones, then slid just below the water to lunge again. But it headed for the mat and came up hard below it. One green flew through the air into the water. Two others were thrown across Tock and Tom. They landed hard. One's head smashed into the side of Tom's face, bruising his eye. Tock was beginning to feel again and wished he couldn't. They lay as they fell, not moving, and heard the swimming green's scream as the flensher lunged after its motion and chopped it in half. Tock realized that the soothing water on his sunburned chest came from the tears of the green person lying on him.

VIII

Deep Regrets

AMANDA FELT the tears running hot on her cheeks and she wanted to hide away somewhere nobody could see her. She was behaving like a baby, and it just made everything worse. She had to stop right now.

"David!" She ordered. "Stand still. You've been acting like a bee-stung weanling ever since we left earth."

David actually did calm down, a little bit and not for long, but he did. He always appreciated firm leadership when he needed it, and he really needed it now. "I know," he apologized. "I can't seem to help it. Keep telling me."

"I can't." Amanda wiped her face fiercely. They were walking down a corridor in the space transport they'd been ferried to from earth. The ferrying itself had been harrowing. The Authority had sedated them heavily so that they could tolerate being strapped down. She was beginning to forget the urge to fight the restraints and the nightmare feeling that she couldn't make her muscles move to escape. She hoped David was forgetting, too.

Right now, however, they both needed a different kind of self-control. Their guide, a long-limbed, small person with an exaggeratedly expressive face and bluish skin, was taking them to their quarters. He had made obsequious efforts to make them comfortable but every overly warm smile just raised the tension. All they had seen felt alien and cold: plastics and metal everywhere; exposed machinery; people of at least a dozen species hurrying urgently or working with great concentration on mysterious tasks. Amanda could not imagine that their living quarters would be anything but grim. Trying to go to the games was turning out to be the worst mistake of her life.

"I can't be responsible for you. I'm having enough trouble of my own," Amanda explained. She was not going to tell him that she couldn't seem to stop crying. David responded with a snort that somehow seemed both sympathetic and disgusted. Amanda thought how accurate and comforting that was for her and David responded as if she had communicated on purpose.

"You're welcome." He said. "I do agree that so far this experience is miserable. At this rate we'll be so stressed and exhausted by the time we get to perform we won't be able to do a thing." Amanda agreed fully.

David had never hurt her in all the eighteen years of her life, but he jigged so jerkily down the corridor, as if he were avoiding invisible intrusions from every direction, that she thought he might tromp on her now.

"If you step on me, I'll kick you back," she threatened. To her relief she found that mustering the necessary hardness for that remark dried her tears. David just laughed to himself, and again managed to calm down briefly, so that when they reached their quarters and the guide turned around to usher them in, they appeared quite composed.

The rooms were perfect. The first was hardly a room at all, more a front yard. It had dirt for the floor, covered in golden, waving grass, with a corral against the far wall enclosing a paddock with a shed and manger. David walked directly over to it and entered through the open gate. The footing was loose, kind of dusty. He lowered his head and snorted, stirring up a small cloud. Slowly he kneeled down, twisting as he lowered, and rolled blissfully in the dirt.

"It's perfect," said Amanda in astonishment. She walked over and closed the gate.

As she watched David roll she felt her face relax. She heard a sound behind her and turned toward her room, which actually looked like the outside of a house. The door stood invitingly open, as did the window beside it. Curtains inside moved as if there were a slight breeze and the multi-colored cat on the windowsill, the source of the noise, stretched and purr-mewed toward her.

"Hey, pussness." Amanda addressed the small animal and quickly established that she loved a good scratch. "Look, David," she called. "Our favorite after-practice relaxer."

The cat jumped down from the sill and sauntered over to David's paddock fence. With an effortless leap it landed on the thin top rail and sat demurely, as if a two-millimeter width of wood were as sumptuous a seat as any easy chair. David moseyed over and bent his nose down to sniff gently at the creature. "I like it. Her." David said. "Shall we name her?"

"Yeah. Something like 'Medicine' or something, because we need her so we won't feel awful." Amanda leaned against the fence herself, idly patting the cat, who was purring loud enough to be heard throughout the room. David brought his nose right next to her and she reached out and placed a paw beside his far nostril as if to hold him in place and licked him twice. His laughter billowed in Amanda's mind. It must have tickled.

"Aspirin," David announced. "Her name is Aspirin." Now it was Amanda's turn to laugh out loud.

"Take two Aspirin and call me in the morning." Aspirin purred and blinked her eyes with pleasure while the horse and the young woman laughed as hard as they could. This felt so much better than crying.

"The Ambassador will be pleased that you like your quarters." Now that they were no longer unhappy the blue guide seemed to have stiffened up.

"This is Asa's design?!" Amanda was astonished.

"I told you he was trying hard," David admonished.

"It's so…so much like home," Amanda explained. He had left to serve the Interplanetary Authority when she was so young that she didn't think of him as knowing much about home or her at all.

"And it's so quiet," David added. The blue man didn't seem to have heard him, so Amanda said something out loud.

"It's much quieter than anywhere we've been since we left our planet. Did you do that on purpose?"

The blue man seemed so pleased they expected him to take personal credit for the serenity. "All the quarters are shielded against sonic and other kinds of waves." He took a deep breath as if he were about to go into a technical explanation, and Amanda found she didn't like him any better as a fussy informant than as an overeager host. David sighed.

"You know, we are quite tired. Even though we haven't done anything in…hours..or maybe even a couple of days. I don't know how to keep track of time here."

Again their guide went into self-satisfied action. "Ah. The time on this transport is universal. If you require rhythmic darkness, there is a voice-activated communicator in your room which will provide that. It will also reserve time for you in the practice area, print directions for getting around the transport and explain the food service." He took a breath to continue and Amanda managed to cut him off.

"That's fine. Thank you. I think we'll just rest a bit now, if you don't mind." Where did that come from, she wondered. She didn't give a fig if he minded and she wouldn't usually pretend that she did. Maybe leaving home had activated some obscure diplomacy genes she shared with her brother. She hoped not.

The guide stiffened a bit, as if he might mind quite a lot no longer being needed. "Fine," he said. "I'll have the screening committee visit you in two universal hours. That's four earth hours." He turned to walk out.

"Screening?" Amanda asked. The guide opened the door and let himself out. At the last minute he popped his head back in.

"To see if you are eligible for the games." He said and disappeared.

IX

Heading To Port

THE CLOSER they got to the port the more Jula worried that somehow she wouldn't be qualified to compete. She tore her lavender trumpet flower into shreds and crumpled them before letting them drop to the ground. They were only another day's travel from the port but the period for establishing eligibility would only last a couple of days longer than that. Nobody else was trying out from this planet. What would she have to do?

"You're supposed to be eating that, not murdering it," Hank pointed out. They had stopped in an open field by a cluster of the flowers to have lunch and to give the smaller members of her joyous escort an overdue rest. Only Hank and Jula stood, and for once she seemed more restless than he did.

Professor was watching her destruction of the plant, too. "It's very high in vitamin C and blue factor," he pointed out.

"How can you be so sure that there's no tryout? You don't even have technology. I know I read something about a screening." Jula felt uncharacteristically like picking a fight.

Hank gave up. "I'm only telling you what the mappers said after they reached the port last year. If you have to worry about something, think about the band of Snatchers tracking us." He turned away to go nestle with the youngest Grounder on the expedition, who had already fallen fast asleep. Jula watched him fold little Carlo into a hug and settle down himself in the soft golden knee high grass. He sure looked like the father of this group to her, no matter what he said.

"Why do you need to do mapping anyway?" She took on Professor, since Hank wouldn't tussle. "There must have been complete aerials of all the land masses before they put the seed populations down for the settlements."

"Plants. Animals. We map the life on the planet."

"Why?" Even Jula could hear that her attitude went beyond stubbornness. Her blues swirled around, not wanting to light on her skin.

Professor looked at her oddly through his old-fashioned glasses. "I have theories I'm trying to prove," he said. Jula stared back, considered pushing him further, but realized that wouldn't relieve her disquiet.

"What's with you anyway?" He asked. "I wouldn't think you'd mind qualifying to get to these precious games of yours. It probably just involves some kind of competition, and you like competing, right?" And when she only sighed for answer, "You're like me. Kind of obsessed. It makes you really good at the one thing that's most important."

"I don't know," she answered. "We have one last push to the river, right? Then a day of building a raft and floating to the port. I should be ecstatic, but I'm scared and itching for a fight. And I have these crazy thoughts."

"Like what?" He sounded genuinely interested. Maggie and a couple of others had told her that Professor collected strange dreams and weird thoughts as if they were pieces of some puzzle.

"Like when I get to the river I'm going to stay in it. Like when I come back from the games nobody will be here anymore. Like the planet wants us to do something. Fast."

That perked him up. "The planet? Any images with that? Anything like a picture?"

She concentrated with her eyes closed. "A tree." She said finally. "Only it's underground and the roots are little and stick out in the air. As if it were upside down. And it's sick or something."

Professor ripped open his pack and rifled through a book of sketches. "A tree like this?" He showed her his drawing of a larrimore, tall thin and stately, with short, quickly tapering branches and no leaves. Jula had called it a stick tree when she had seen one camping with her family as a child. She had thought it was dead. The drawing showed below the ground as well, where the roots curved and branched like regular limbs, making much wider and more complicated patterns than above.

"That's it," Jula agreed. "It looks upside down. But how did you know about the part the ground hides?"

"One blew over." Professor stared at the picture. In fact he stared so hard she gave up on the conversation and headed off into the field to practice dancing.

She hadn't danced much since going to ground, but the minute she started she realized that her blues were actually doing more than ever, helping with every move, flowing farther past her fingertips and beyond her pointed toes. She usually practiced everything at half speed because that made it so much harder and took so much control, but today she went full tilt into one of the earliest pieces she and her blues had made together. The workout felt wonderful.

Hooting and clapping sounded from the direction of the lunch stopover and she looked up from her final pose to see Maggie, Carlo and several others hunkered down watching her. Carlo imitated several of her moves out of sheer exuberance, causing his huggy to climb his head and cling there to keep from falling. "That was great!" He beamed. "Teach me how. Please, please?" Jula suddenly thought how much teaching the children did of each other. No wonder she kept thinking of them as a family. Carlo bounced and skipped around her.

"Save some of that energy," she laughed. "We're going to be walking a lot before dark."

Suddenly Carlo calmed down and he and the others looked serious. "Maybe, maybe not," Maggie told her. "Professor and Hank are talking about it."

"They're fighting," Carlo insisted. He obviously disapproved of this. Nobody looked happy.

"Let's go see," she suggested.

Carlo danced along beside Jula as full of energy now as he had been sound asleep earlier. "Will you be my new mama?" He asked her.

"Wouldn't your real mama mind that?" Jula responded.

"She's dead," he said matter of factly. "She had an accident and she told the doctor not to send her away, so she died." He accepted the hard rule of pioneering, choose technical medicine and leave the planet for good or stay and take your chances with what had been developed in your new home.

"What about your dad?" Jula wondered.

"I heard him making plans to leave so I had to go to ground early." Carlo sounded sad and Jula thought that explained his preference for being close to Hank. She let him take her hand and wondered at how good it felt.

"Maggie," Hank called out. "We need you to send a message. Professor?"

"Ask the mappers where they've seen larrimore trees and are any of them sick?"

Maggie held out her arm and her warbler walked down from her shoulder to perch on her forefinger. She stared at him and said, "Listen." He cocked his small white head as if obeying and Maggie whistled in a complicated way for what seemed like minutes.

"Repeat," she commanded. This was clearly more complex than the parlor trick of greeting her twin. The bird sang back at her too long for Jula to recognize it all, though she did catch some phrases. "Okay," Maggie nodded and held the bird aloft where it sang a loud full-throated melody then repeated the long message at full volume.

The Grounders sat and waited silently, Professor tense with worry, Hank more serious than ever, Jula full to bursting with unasked questions. It went on so long that some of them started braiding grasses for ropes and baskets. Finally they heard a long faint birdsong from the direction they knew the Snatchers were in. Maggie's warbler walked excitedly up and down her forearm, then turned to her and sang the answer.

Maggie nodded and said, "Repeat. Slow." Jula thought Professor might burst from frustration, but when Maggie spoke she turned to Hank.

"The mappers are four days over there. There are two larrimores, maybe more, between them and us. The Snatchers are between us, too. The trees were healthy when they saw them, but now they see smoke from that direction."

"Smoke!" Professor wailed.

Maggie went on. "They think the Snatchers torched one of the trees."

Professor was frantic. "We have to go back! We have to put it out! We have to! The whole thing will burn! We have to go back! Now!"

"Quiet," Hank commanded. "I promised Jula we would get her to the port in time. You can go on toward the tree without us."

"No. We need you. We have to figure out how to put it out. Now." Professor started to cry big tears that just rolled down his face. Hank looked hard, but he wasn't meeting anybody's eye.

"We need you to protect us," Maggie said, referring to the Snatchers.

"If you had to, you could ask my folks for help," Jula heard herself say to Professor. "My dad sounds tough, but he's okay, and my mom tried to make snatching illegal last year."

"No! We need you to protect our home," Professor choked out still to Hank. "There isn't time to get her to the port and put out the fire, too."

Hank looked at Jula and suddenly everyone else did, too. With a dreadful certainty she realized she would have to choose whether to go or stay.

X

The Campfire

JOSH FIGURED their choice was either to make a run for it tonight, or delay and risk running out of time to make it to the port. The three soldiers who had joined them earlier sat closer to the fire than Josh and Cor. The two of them rested together with their backs to a rock far enough away to keep all the others in view. The smell of roasting game and smoke was strong, maybe strong enough to attract a falcon patrol, Josh thought. He hadn't forbidden the fire because he wanted the men to sleep soundly, and they were too thin to stay warm without it.

Squints peered at them over a half-gnawed bone. "Not as juicy as he'd be, but not bad."

"Ain't you heard not to eat the milk cow, fool?" Jesser demanded rhetorically. "He's a better hunter than any ol' hand hawk I ever seen." Jesser always seemed to have the last word, and apparently he had decided he had his own reasons for honoring Josh's order not to harm Cor.

Fielder finally spoke for the first time since the trio had found them. "He's not even marked as a prisoner." His voice was empty and cold. Josh wondered how there could be so much menace in so few words, and Cor fought to keep himself from attack-screaming. Jesser might lead, but Fielder was the real threat.

"Now you're the fool," Jesser answered, though with less confidence than he showed against Squints. "Rip his flight feathers out to mark him, cripple him for hunting."

Fielder stayed quiet, but kept staring at Cor. Josh wondered if he might have figured out they were imposters or whether he just couldn't stand the sight of a healthy, unmarked enemy. The darkness deepened and the fire began to shrink down to embers. The men arranged themselves for sleep curled with their backs to the fire for warmth. Josh was taking the first watch.

More urgent than deciding whether to escape was figuring out how and where to empty his churning bowels. He waited as long as he could and finally spoke to Cor. "I have to go. I think they're asleep. They'll never know." Cor shifted slightly as if he were going to protest, but Josh forestalled him. "If they wake up and notice, say I heard something and went to check it out. I really have to go." He faded into the dark quickly and silently. He wouldn't go far, just far enough for the smallest bit of privacy. Cor sympathized. Part of the debasement of war, he had realized, was never being able to eliminate in a decent way.

Cor closed his eyes. He wished he could sleep. He wished he were back in Cavernhome. He wished he knew how close they were to the port. The swirl of thoughts cleared immediately when he heard Fielder speak to Jesser.

"You could mark him. You know how. So he'll still be able to hunt."

"Go to sleep. He'd never let us do it." Jesser didn't sound sleepy, just like he didn't want trouble. Cor felt danger. Fielder sat up and got close to Jesser. Without his great hearing Cor wouldn't have been able to hear him wheedle.

"Come on. He's gone. You know how," Fielder pushed. "You're better than anyone with hawks. Just a couple of feathers. You know which ones. And he won't be able to get away or fly far, just enough to keep hunting. Come on. We'll mark him and burn the feathers as a war trophy." Cor knew it was true. If Jesser knew how, he could take out key pinions and cripple him for distance. And they'd never be able to fly at the games. But Cor couldn't kill them all by himself. He wasn't sure he could bring himself to kill any of them. If Jesser came after him to pluck him, he would have to stand for it without defending himself, as if he really were a helpless prisoner.

Where Josh crouched behind a boulder in the dark he couldn't hear any of the furtive whispering around the fire. He could see a glow from that direction, a perfect target for a heatseeker, if there were falcon patrols in the area. He rose to return to the camp and heard loose pebbles rattle in the distance. Stiff with concentration he listened for more. If there were falcons walking, that's the kind of sound they would make, and their night vision wasn't any better than his own, so they wouldn't be flying.

Another pebble clattered. They were still far enough away, but getting closer. Josh circled outward to try to put the patrol between him and the campsite. He grinned ruefully – he was doing just what he had told Cor, checking out a noise. Be careful what lies you set up, he thought to himself. They may come true. He felt grateful for the training that had made him take his weapons with him, hopeful that he wouldn't have to kill anyone to save Cor.

Josh moved as silently as the best night hunter. In fact, he almost cried out when he stepped so close to something that it slithered around his booted foot and disappeared between rocks. His heart pounded loud in his ears. He decided to stop where he was till he could get a bead on the patrol by sound again. He stood loosely in a stance he could hold almost forever and waited for his heart to quiet. After a while he realized that he didn't hear the patrol any more. He had a sense of where they were, but not because of anything he could name. He concentrated in that general area.

Perhaps it was the years of growing up around falcons that allowed him to hear the short phrase pitched out of the usual human range of voices. "Got 'em," the falcon announced. They had spotted the campsite.

Josh had to think fast. A falcon patrol would liberate Cor. They would kill the soldiers. Nobody tried to take prisoners at night. They had spotted the fire, so they would know not to shoot until they could aim directly for the people. A wild shot now would just hit the embers. The soldiers might suffer a few burns, but they'd have time to scatter.

Josh raised his arm with the heatseeker attached and fired into the sky. The projectile wouldn't find its target till its descent. He hoped he had aimed high enough to bypass the falcon patrol.

Light erupted from the campsite where the projectile exploded in the fire. He heard the yells of the men and the closer swearing of the falcons.

"Go in! Find whatever's moving and shoot it. No, wait! Smell. There's a raptor. Find the raptor." Josh wondered how they could smell Cor at this distance and then the unmistakable scent of burned feathers reached him. He felt sick. His plan to save the soldiers must have hurt Cor somehow.

The falcon patrol moved fast and Josh followed them. He could relax about the human soldiers, anyway. They'd get as far from the campsite as they could as fast as possible. Was Cor all right? Would they find him?

Josh couldn't get close enough to see what happened, but the patrol was talking loudly to each other. They, too, knew that hitting the fire had scattered any threat in every direction. They would never imagine that they were being shadowed by one lone soldier who had no thought of fighting, just the wish to reunite with one of their number.

"Hey! You okay?" They had found Cor.

"It's an officer!" He must still be in pretty good shape.

"Well, well. Higher ranking than me. Welcome to the Flight, sir. You seem to be our new commander." Then Josh heard a sound that made him feel more alone than he could ever have imagined. The falcons laughed. Not with the soft humanlike chuckling he was used to, but with the screechy rasp of birds who had never known any but their own kind.

XI

Recovering

It felt good to laugh again after the flenshers had moved on. In fact, though they all still felt sad over the green who had died, at the moment Tom was floating helplessly on his back, giggling too hard to swim. One of their new friends was in a similar fix. They had been playing school as they swam toward the port city in order to help Tock loosen up and get rid of the residual effects of the paralyzing toxins, and the last school leader had made them do a sequence of moves none of them could really accomplish. They had all been watching at the end when Tock had tried and failed hilariously.

"Here's Tock," called out one of the group. He spread his arms sideways as rigid as boards, surged out of the water and fell to the left, and again, falling this time to the right, finally spurting up out of the water completely stiff and executing a perfect half somersault, so that he flopped down in the water flat on his back. The laughter resumed.

"My turn to lead," called out the quickly improving Tock. He swam strongly past all the good-natured kidding and took his place at the front of the group. He arced up in a shallow crescent above the surface, nothing showy, but supple and clean, then dived into the water. When the green people realized that he must be doing his maneuvers underwater, they followed quickly.

Tom went first, not because there was any real order to follow, but because he was used to Tock's thinking and realized right away that his friend was making the game harder by doing it all beneath the surface. They had played this way for years, ever since he'd been assigned to Tock at his studies. Sometimes Tock had suggested they play after a particularly difficult day, when Tom had tried his hardest to keep up, yet hadn't. Equals in the water, they could work off their complementary frustrations, giving their all physically and staying together, rather than having Tock pull ahead or Tom fall behind. In the water there was no resentment over anyone's intelligence. In the water there was no envy of clever fingers that could make great ideas real.

Tom saw when he dove that Tock was spiraling down in a tightening circle. They enjoyed this one and sometimes did it in interlocking unison. He went deep before squirting fast toward the surface. Tom realized Tock must be feeling much better and guessed he was testing his breath control and stamina.

By the end of the sequence Tock and Tom rested on the surface and watched the rest of the green people attempt the air work Tock had invented as the final set of moves. It consisted of a double flip with one twist and splash-free, sharp reentry. A couple of the green people got it right, but most got completely disorganized in mid-air and fell in a heap to their own great amusement.

"Pat and Kip must be wave dancers," Tom said.

"They certainly are better than the others," Tock agreed. Then, "Hey! Who'd this?" Tom followed his gaze and saw that another dolphin had joined them and was bringing up the rear, trying to follow Tock's lead. It was a good try, too, with clean flips and a full twist, but a splat of an entry.

"Almost," Tock called out to the newcomer. "We're making the game hard so that I can get over being poisoned by drifters." The dolphin swam closer, ringed quickly by the curious heads of the green people.

"How did you manage to survive?" The dolphin asked. She was older, as they could all see once they got a good look, and Tom had the feeling he had met her before, but he couldn't place where. "I am guessing that these good people had something to do with your excellent fortune."

"They had everything to do with it, Your Grace," Tock answered. He obviously knew she was important. Maybe he recognized her. "If they had not lifted me onto a raft of matweed, I'd have been flensher food."

"He saved us too, though," Pat offered generously. "He's the one who thought of getting on the mat in the first place," Pat didn't give her a title. Green people didn't have titles, so they usually didn't bother, even with very powerful or knowledgeable dolphins.

She didn't seem to mind the omission. "I'm Oshi of Deep Sea," she offered. "The world council sent me to vouch for the team we are entering in the interspecies games. When they get to the port city they will need some help with the formalities of getting offworld. I think I'm behind them by a tide, but I never could resist a good game of school."

Don't worry, ma'am," Tom answered happily. "You're in the exact right spot. That's me and Tock, that team you're talking about." The greens were as astonished as Oshi. They knew they were headed for the port, but in typical green fashion they hadn't bothered to find out why any more than they would have thought of going back to their own business before making sure Tock had recovered fully.

"Hey, algae face," Pat said to Tom. "I thought you could swim pretty well. I was going to ask you to wave dance later, but I should have guessed you already have a partner."

"Yeah, my poddy's not bad for a half-fish with no tail," Tock admitted. His expressive face showed his love and pride.

Oshi brought them all back to serious matters. "I am very grateful you survived the drifter poisoning. Do you feel you'll be able to do your best for the planet?" Tock thought she was asking about his mental abilities, not just his physical well-being.

"Yes, ma'am. I think so." Then to make sure, he checked with Tom. "Have I seemed odd to you since the poisoning? You know, kind of slow?"

Tom cocked his head. It was tempting to make a joke, but he didn't out of respect for the councilwoman. "Slow? Like me?" He asked in all honesty. "No. You're the same old Tock. You still think too much." He finally smiled, very glad to be able to say it.

Oshi took over and led the group in a slightly different direction. Going as they had Tom and Tock would have had to fight the current on their final approach to the port. As on every planet the port was a land base enclosed to minimize its chemical, technological and ecological impact. Here on this world of vast seas some water surrounding the port's island was enclosed as well to allow the intelligent water dwellers to approach it. Most of the inhabitants would live their whole lives having nothing to do with the place, aware of its traffic to and from space, electing representatives to the Council who would foster distant friendliness with the port inhabitants and keep them irrelevant to everyday life.

The greens only wanted to go as far as the enclosing wall, not into the port itself.

"Do you really have to leave the planet completely, you poor things?"

"Are you sure you want to do this?"

"Do those people have enough water where they live?"

"Will they let you stay together the whole time?"

"Won't you be lonely?"

The questions came in a stream too thick to allow any answers. They bothered Tom a bit. He had been wondering how they would get wherever it was the games were to be held, and he could not imagine being separated from Tock. If that was part of this deal, he might rethink his willingness to go along with the whole scheme, rescue mission or no rescue mission. Tock answered that doubt in just the right way.

"I don't know how they plan to transport us, though it will certainly have to be in some amount of our water, which they can reproduce, I'm sure, and we will be together the whole time, because we will insist on it." He looked around with piercing dolphin intensity, as if challenging anyone listening to see just how insistent they could be.

Oshi had been listening carefully. She approved of what she was hearing very much, and when she answered, she was speaking to everyone there but thinking of her colleagues who still had doubts. "I'm sure there won't be any problem," she stated. "I've been authorized to negotiate your conditions and to introduce you to all the right people. Let's proceed."

The greens hugged Tom good-bye and stroked Tock like old friends. They had no idea that the future of the whole planet rested with these two, but it wouldn't have mattered much to them, if they had known. Just taking leave from people they liked and wishing them well in the unknown would have been more important to their warm, uncomplicated hearts.

Tom and Tock followed Oshi inside the port enclosure, where the water was as still as the most protected lagoon and just a bit too warm for comfort. “I hope they don’t think this is how cool we like it,” Tock muttered anxiously.

“Don’t worry, poddy,” Tom offered, speaking as much to himself as Tock. “We’ll do all right. There’s nothing the two of us can’t handle together.”

XII

The Answer

Amanda needed to feel closer to David, to remind herself that they were handling this together. She didn't like having the visitor between her and him, even if she could almost see through it, whatever it was. It shimmered in the air between them, making fleeting colored shards of light. David seemed to be fascinated by it. He strained his neck over the fence of his enclosure and tried to sniff it. Amanda could see it pulled toward him and pushed away as David snuffed and exhaled in greeting. She didn't think it looked like anything with a sense of smell, so she doubted it would understand the horse graciousness of exchanging breath smells as an introduction. She doubted that it would understand much of anything, but mostly she just wanted it to go somewhere else, so that it wasn't separating her from David.

"Would you mind standing, or being, or whatever it is you do, somewhere other than in between us?" Amanda addressed the shimmer.

"Oh, sorry. Of course," she was amazed to hear. The thing had a very nice, soothing voice. It floated over by the gate into David's paddock. Amanda wondered what this thing was that she had let into their quarters. And for that matter however had it managed to knock at their door?

The shimmer giggled. "Actually, I can make any noise." It demonstrated by knocking again and then by neighing exactly as David might to call to a neighboring pasture. David tossed his head in astonishment and swung his nose over to sniff it again.

"And you can read any mind, too, I take it." Amanda noted sourly.

"Oh, sorry," it apologized immediately. "You seem to be telepathic, at least with this being here, so I thought you wouldn't mind. I hope I haven't offended you."

David finally entered the discussion. "You are very calming," he told it. "Unlike many of the other beings we have met since we've been here."

"Thank you," it answered. "I do try, and that's a very nice compliment coming from you."

"What are you supposed to find out about us?" Amanda asked. "I mean, I assume you're the screener or part of the committee or something."

"No committee, just me," it answered. "I have to check everybody out to make sure both the species in a pair are intelligent." Amanda stiffened and felt her throat constrict. This was what she had hoped for all along, a test to bring back to the doubters on earth to prove that humans were not the only intelligent species on the planet. The silence extended. David seemed so relaxed as to be almost drowsy. Aspirin stretched where she slept on the chair on the porch, then curled up again. Amanda couldn't make herself ask. Now would be a good time for this screener thing to read her mind.

The screener giggled again. "Don't worry. You're in." Then it addressed David, though how Amanda could tell it was doing that was beyond her. "I can see why she's good for you. That's a very strong will."

"Yes," David answered. "I appreciate that. But what do you mean by saying that it's good for me?"

"Don't you know?" The shimmer asked.

"No. All I know is that I can understand her and I don't understand much of anybody. You are an obvious exception."

"Ah." The shimmer seemed to consolidate itself in mid air. Amanda guessed it was thinking.

"Do you know why David doesn't seem to understand other people?" She asked. "Does it have anything to do with how jumpy he was on the way here?" She shied away from asking for an explanation of their performance back on earth, which had been such a disaster she didn't let herself think about it for fear of crying again. It had been the first time ever that she had fallen off David's back, and though they covered the flub well by changing their routine, she had felt ashamed and unworthy every since.

"Yes, I do know why he can't understand others. And it probably explains his jumpiness completely," the shimmer said. "He is very receptive to all sorts of beings. You may be a universal receiver," it said to David as an aside. "But there is a problem with will. If the sender's will is mixed, if they are in conflict about what they want or what they are trying to do, he can't make sense of it. Most humans can't be clear enough for him to read. In fact, he may become rather confused himself by all the noise of conflicted effort."

"So I'm clear when I know what I want," Amanda thought it made sense. "But why did you say that I was good for David?"

"You don't have any choice about reading the wills around you," the shimmer told him. "If you were in your natural setting, which is a group living situation, you would monitor the wills around you at all times."

David stood taller, as if at attention, and nodded. "In the herd. Of course. That explains a great deal."

"And having a clear, firm will in a trusted companion allows you to relax and stop monitoring so hard. It's probably restful." David agreed with the shimmer immediately. "You are somewhat receptive as well," it continued to Amanda. "But I doubt that it bothers you much, because your concentration on him is excellent."

Amanda felt strange and light all at the same time. Something about this way of looking at David made her almost giddy with happiness. That was the light part. Finally having such a fine answer for all the skeptics who thought him a "dumb beast of burden" let her put down guards she didn't even know she had up. That's what was so strange. It had been years she'd been fighting this fight for him, for them. The shimmer continued talking to David, promising him a special shield for walking around the ship, so that he wouldn't have to bother hearing everybody's indecipherable confusions and ambivalences. Amanda felt exhausted. She thought she might be able to sleep for five days.

"I would like your permission to turn to you for help reading other species, if the need should arise," the shimmer said to David on its way out of their quarters.

"Sure," David said with some surprise. "Will you mind, Amanda?" He asked. She just smiled.

"Why not? This family has always worked in interplanetary diplomacy." Amanda felt the deepest satisfaction she could imagine. No matter what happened now this whole effort had been a success.

XIII

Family Support

The little ones in the group could hardly stay awake. Carlo aimed himself for a patch of moss and fell so hard he almost bounced. They had pushed on relentlessly till dusk, just reaching the river's broad ford as the light faded. Now on the far side, the tree side as Professor kept saying, all but Jula and Hank sat or lay down the moment they stopped walking. Jula thought Hank could go on forever, but even though she had a dancer's stamina, she felt that she, too, would be asleep as soon as she shut her eyes.

Hank peered downstream and inland and walked restlessly around the group. He singled Maggie out and put a hand on her shoulder. His greens flowed beyond his fingertips and Jula knew that where they lay Maggie would feel a light, comforting warmth. She looked up at him, tired but trusting.

"Maggie, we don't have enough riverdogs to camp this close to the water." Not with Maggie's warbler attracting sneels, anyway. "I want you to take the expedition inland to the first stand of trees and make nests for the little ones. We'll be back after moonrise. I'm going downstream with Jula to see where we can tap the river, if Professor's right."

"I'm right," Professor said grimly. "The tree's burning underground just like the old peat bogs on earth. I just don't know what else is going to be affected. I haven't worked out the relationships yet." He looked haunted and even more exhausted than the others. Still, he somehow seemed to mean it when he pleaded, "Let me go with you."

"No." Hank was uncharacteristically stern. For a minute he reminded Jula of her mother, accommodating till the need arose and then stony strong. "You're too tired. We'll need you fresh in the morning to help engineer getting the water to the tree. Jula's still got miles in her. We're just going to find a good spot."

She doubted she had miles in her at all. She couldn't imagine they'd be able to see much in the growing dark. But ever since she had decided to give up going to the games, so that they would all be free to help with the fire, she hadn't said much and she didn't voice her objections now. She didn't feel sad, exactly, just kind of flat and strange inside, though she didn't question her decision. She looked at all her new friends and thought I got the big family I always wanted.

Hank moved out and she followed. Even in the poor visibility of dusk before moonrise he moved fast and she realized quickly she would have to concentrate to keep up. He followed the river closely and it made a kind of darker emptiness on the right side, something felt and heard more than seen.

Soon they began to go slightly uphill as the bank rose and the river narrowed to a deeper channel. Then they were slowed by undergrowth. Somehow Hank maintained a walking pace, but Jula had to stay closer not to lose him.

"This is the river that would have taken you to the port," he commented. Jula only grunted in reply. Tomorrow they would be figuring out how to get the river's water to the burning tree, not making a raft to carry them to the port city.

"Are you sorry? That you decided to stay?" Hank persisted.

"No." Jula sounded more curt than she wanted to. "It wasn't even a question really." Though it wasn't that simple either. "I'm not sorry I stayed. I'm just sorry not to be going to the games. If that makes any sense to you."

"Oh, yes. Perfect sense." Hank seemed satisfied in some way and Jula was relieved that he didn't want to talk any more.

They broke out of the dense growth onto a moonlit meadow stretching down to the shimmering ribbon of the river. The moon was only a width above the horizon, but it illuminated everything, even casting shadows from the driftwood logs and boulders at the water's edge.

"Perfect," Hank declared. He headed straight for the river.

"What are you looking for?" Jula asked.

"Someplace where we can wade in without getting swept away, and where the water we pipe out doesn't have to go uphill to go inland." The meadow seemed to stretch forever, so they had the latter feature. "Want to go for a swim?" He asked her.

"I don't know how," Jula confessed.

"I'll teach you someday," he answered, not slowing for a minute. "Okay, come here." He squatted to pick up one end of a huge log and carry it into the river, where he dropped it with a splash.

"Whatever are you doing?" she asked.

"Checking to make sure we can work in the river. I need you to go out to the end of the log while I hold it perpendicular to the bank. See what kind of strength it takes."

This made vague sense to her, and when he held out his hand to help her onto the log she gave him hers. His greens spread onto her arm. It felt warm, but also odd and she looked back at him, but he urged her on.

"Keep going. Out to that end. I'll be holding this one in place." He waded in as she balanced along its length. It bobbled and wobbled as she reached the end some forty feet into the river and she crouched down to keep her balance. It gave a funny lurch and she fell to her hands and knees. Then she looked back. Hank was a dark silhouette in the water at the end of the log, which was floating free. As she watched he seemed to stretch out his arms and it began to leave him, slowly arcing to point down river.

"Hey!" She yelled. "What are you doing?!" And in a flash she knew. This was her raft. What she had felt on her fingertips when he took her hand was a good-bye kiss.

"You'll do great at the games," he yelled back.

"How am I supposed to get to shore when I can't swim?" She screamed.

Hank just laughed. He cupped his hands so his voice would carry to her. "When you get to the port, use your blues and fly."

XIV

Marked By War

"I can't fly that far." From where he hid crouched behind the boulder Josh heard Cor say those words with a deep sadness that told him they must be true.

"Why not?" The falcon Lieutenant asked. Then less brashly, as befitted his rank, "You don't seem to be injured, sir."

"They marked me," Cor answered, unfolding his wings to show where Jesser had pulled the long flight feathers he would need for balance in all but the shortest flights. "Pulled them and burned them. They said they liked the stink."

"Looks like they knew what they were doing," the Lieutenant noted. "Keep you airborne for small game but crippled for getting away."

Josh stared into the distance at the intergalactic port. As the light faded into dusk here in the scrublands, the lights under the port dome began to twinkle. It looked beautiful, and so exotic in this place of war where anything handmade was hidden to protect its maker, human or falcon. Josh's heart broke, slowly and forever, as he realized that he and Cor would never be able to fly at the games.

"Too bad," the Lieutenant continued. "The air space is safe this close to the port. We could have made good time. When we get to headquarters, we'll get you some implants." He spread his own right wing to show the synthetic feathers there. "Half of these are surgeon's artwork. Great stuff. So light they have to weight them to balance the natural wing. Never molt. You'll be good as new in no time, Colonel." Cor didn't answer.

Josh heard them shuffle away. He knew he should move, take advantage of the twilight to track back to his water before it was too dark to ensure silence. But he could not take his eyes off the far, twinkling dome of the port. Everything felt dead heavy and empty and dried out, as if he might never be able to move again but would just crack and crumble to dust in the next day's desert heat.

Slowly he realized that he had not injured Cor with his heatseeking blast into the campfire, as he had feared. The stink of burning feathers had come from the humans' grim prisoner of war ritual. He should feel relieved. He should be glad that Cor would fly again and hadn't been grounded forever by their brutality. Perhaps he should even be glad that they were both still alive, but he wasn't. All he could feel was that the mission was lost. They would never be accepted to compete with prosthetics. They would never be able to show the worlds what the strength of peace looked like.

He heard the little dusk creatures begin to stir and the breeze picked up enough to rustle a quakebush. Still he could not move. Nor could he tear his gaze from the port. So close. So close. Not even a morning's walk from where he crouched. He knew they would never compete. He knew they had no more reason to reach the port. But somehow he could not give it up. With every hollow breath left to him he would strive to reunite with Cor and to reach the port. Even if it made no sense, he would keep on. He would keep on, because if he did not, he knew he would die. Josh stood to go.

A coney skittered twelve feet to his left and a grand falcon fell from the sky on it. The bird of prey shrieked softly in triumph, then snorted and whipped its head in his direction. Scented!

"Enemy! Enemy! Here force! Here force!" The hunting falcon called to the others. Josh thought fast.

"I have no weapon except this heatseeker. See? I'm dropping it. I'm unarmed. I surrender." Josh held his hands high.

The falcon flapped once and landed in front of him. He reached out with the talons of one foot and pulled the heatseeker to him. "That was stupid, brownass. Now I can have something better for dinner than that coney." Slowly he picked the heatseeker up to transfer it to the hand at the end of one wing. The wings themselves stayed flared, at the ready for a disabling blow if Josh moved. He had miscalculated. This falcon would not take him back to camp alive where Cor could try to protect him. He saw the heatseeker's barrel rising toward his chest. He wondered if he would hear it or just die.

"I'm worth more alive to you than dead, vulture." The falcon smashed his right wing into the side of Josh's head, sending him sprawling.

"He's right." Blood from a cut on Josh's forehead blurred his vision, but his ears knew that was Cor who spoke. Josh almost smiled. "He's worth a lot more as a prisoner than as meat," Cor continued.

"You know him?" the Lieutenant sounded surprised. He had some sense that something wasn't right here.

"He's the son of one of the Old Guard, the real thing, from Canyon City. Look at his fitness. You know he's been fed when others haven't." Cor was giving him one of the identities they had developed for just such a situation.

What's he doing this far from home?" The Lieutenant didn't believe him. Cor was silent. Too long, Josh thought.

"Tracking him," Josh said with as much hatred as he could put into his voice.

"Vengelust?" The Lieutenant still wasn't convinced. "Why would he ever surrender? Why not die within shot of you?" Cor roused himself now and came over to Josh. He hooked a talon through the prone human's belt and yanked him across the ground, rough treatment, but nothing hurtful.

"He surrendered to get closer to me." Cor swept the ground with Josh once again. "He thought he might get another chance at me, if he could get close enough." He released Josh with a little push that helped him sit upright. Josh wiped his face and realized he probably looked more injured than he was.

The Lieutenant walked over. Josh could see now that there were four regular troops as well as the officer, all at least half a head smaller than Cor. They should be more afraid of him, because he was bigger. He must not have established his authority. What was wrong with him? Maybe he was as crushed as Josh about the death of their dream of flying in the games.

"Stand, prisoner," the Lieutenant ordered. Josh stood. "Have you sworn vengelust on this officer?" There was utter silence. Even the night seemed to hold its breath.

"If I die, Cor dies with me," Josh stated flatly. He hoped the soldiers would take his statement as a threat. He saw Cor raise his neck feathers, but he was unprepared for the scream that came from his beak. Josh knew his friend had understood the offer he was making and he knew this scream, which the others would take for defiance, was Cor's agonized agreement. They could not fly together, but they could still die together.

Cor's scream faded into the night, and the other grand falcons accepted the situation. The hunter came forward with bindwire. "Put your hands behind you," he ordered. Josh obeyed and felt his wrists encircled. He tried not to move, knowing that the artificial rope they used would shrink with every stretch to the point where it could cut through his wrists entirely.

Another soldier finally spoke. "One coney, six beaks. At least we have the pleasure of watching him starve while we eat." Josh heard Cor take a breath, but nothing was said.

"Wait," the Lieutenant ordered. "Mark him, Colonel." Silence. Nobody moved. "He's your prisoner. Mark him." The air felt tight, even though the night was cooling by the minute.

"He's worth more intact," Cor started, then realized that they would never hold for ransom a soldier who had sworn vengelust. "He has information. He needs to have his stupid head intact for headquarters to squeeze the information out."

"All right. I'm not saying you disable him. Just put your mark on him. An officer of your experience must have put your mark on many a plucked chest." With that the Lieutenant took Josh's collar in his beak and ripped his shirt down to his waist, exposing his left shoulder. Josh's heart raced with fear. That beak so close to his heart! It had been meant to terrify him and it had. He must not let it show. What was Cor waiting for? He must respond.

The Lieutenant turned a cold eye on Cor, almost fleering him, though that would have called for punishment from a commanding officer. He knew something wasn't right. Josh willed Cor to steel himself and do what he had to do.

Cor's own gaze turned to ice as he met the Lieutenant's challenging stare. Staring back the whole time, he reached out, grabbed Josh's belt again and pulled him to his knees. Josh tried to make it look rougher than it was. Now there was no turning back. Cor held him in place with one foot and reached out with the hand at the end of one wing. His sharp-clawed pointer finger traced a "C" above Josh's left nipple. Blood oozed from it and began to drip.

The soldiers were excited. "He's a juicy one," said the hunter. Cor and the Lieutenant still stared at each other, as Cor released Josh with a push.

"Aren't you going to set the scar?" asked the Lieutenant.

Cor drew himself up and flared his crown feathers, till he towered over the others. "Do it yourself, if you want." And he turned haughtily and walked away.

The soldiers shuffled and snickered until one of them said, "Let me, let me."

"Go ahead, then," the Lieutenant responded impatiently. He had lost the unspoken part of his contest with Cor, and he did not seem satisfied by getting what he had asked for out loud.

The soldier grunted and flicked his tail, then stepped aside to reveal a white mess on the ground next to Josh. "Untie his hands," he ordered, and the one who had been hunting did so. Josh was relieved. Being shoved around had shrunk his bonds and he chafed his wrists hard to restore circulation.

"Stop that. Rub it in," the Lieutenant ordered. Josh stooped, dipped two fingers in the guano and rubbed it into the wound on his chest. He gasped at how much it hurt. The soldiers laughed. He thought about the humans who had plucked Cor and how they had probably laughed, too.

"More! More!" cried the one who had provided the acid mess burning its way into Josh's flesh.

"Enough. Retie him. Return to camp." The Lieutenant had lost interest. Josh was glad the sorry band had enough discipline to obey their officer and not to hurt a prisoner with another's mark. He would live this night and sleep closer to Cor.

XV

Making Friends

"I CAN'T SLEEP," Tom complained. "The water doesn't smell right and it's not big enough, and I wish I were at home." He sighed deeply, exhaled and pinched his nostrils shut in disapproval. He lounged half on the platform that sloped into the water of their quarters aboard the space village created for the athletes. One arm and a leg trailed into the calm liquid. Even his splashing back and forth had a dismal quality to it.

"I know. Me, too," Tock tried to comfort him. Their quarters probably were adequate for everything but hunting and practicing, he thought, and they didn't really need to hunt, since fish got released into their swimming space at the press of a button. What impressed Tock more than anything was the fact that Tom was complaining. He considered it symptomatic of how disoriented they were. He tried logic again.

"You heard me talk to that concierge guy who greeted us."

"The blue one?" Tom asked. "I didn't like him very much."

"Yes. The chemist he's sending will figure out the smell problem. They can't do anything about the space itself. I guess this place is packed with species."

"It never occurred to me that so many of them would be land creatures. Did you ever hear the story of how the walkers learned to swim?"

"No. Is that one of the ones you tell your young?" Tock realized he could probably improve Tom's mood by telling him a story, but his own mood wasn't good enough to take that on. For now anyway, grumpy togetherness would have to do.

The entrance to their quarters made a clicking noise and a voice spoke. "The attaché and Dr. Anders are here to see you. May we come in?"

"Of course," Tock answered. Tom slid into the water and swam out a bit to put Tock between himself and the visitors. Irrepressibly friendly and upbeat, Tom was reacting to homesickness with something very close to shyness and melancholy.

The blue man who had greeted them on their arrival came in first. Tom had the urge to splash water all over him just to see his ridiculous fake dignity and pretense of warmth dissolve. After him waddled a short, squat biped with a large head covered in hair the same reddish tan color as his wrinkled skin. He made the impression of being heavy, almost of being connected to the ground through his wide flat feet. The blue man held up a hand in greeting, then seemed embarrassed when he realized that Tock had no way of returning the gesture. Tock smiled and Tom and Dr. Anders exchanged brief waves of acknowledgement.

The blue man tried to make himself shorter as he stood at the water's edge to make introductions. "Tock and Tom of Deepsea, it is my honor to present Dr. Anders of the Guild of Planet 483. He will help you to regulate your environment to be more agreeable, ah, olfactorily. That is, I believe that's the issue." The three were sizing each other up and nobody spoke immediately, causing the blue man no end of consternation. "Can I get you anything to make you more comfortable? Perhaps you would like refreshments? Fish? Something to drink? Ha, ha." He subsided in a misery of self-consciousness.

Tom couldn't stand it any longer. Besides, he wanted to get a better look at this Anders person, so he swam up to the dry slope, carefully pushing a wave ahead of him just toward the feet of the blue man, who stepped back with gratifying swiftness. Tock chuckled. Anders watched this display with clever little eyes that seemed to miss nothing.

"You may go now," Anders seemed to address the blue man as an underling of some kind.

"Of course, of course," the attaché effused. "Just be in touch if you need anything, anything at all." And he left with obvious relief.

Tock and Tom laughed briefly, not a mean laugh, just enjoying having rid themselves of the silly fellow. Dr. Anders was silent, observing them constantly.

"Well, Doctor," Tock addressed him. "Have you biological or chemical expertise that will remedy our sorry condition?"

"Yes and yes," the Doctor answered. "What is your own theory of what might be wrong?" The question seemed almost like a test.

"It smells like piss in here," Tom offered bluntly.

Tock smiled and explained. "There is some scent of waste, though not of any of its unhealthful elements. It is as if our quarters were eliminating just the necessary constituents of our…eliminations." He grinned at his pun. "And leaving the rest. Unfortunately, we are aware of those harmless constituents and find them offensive."

"Hmmph. An apt hypothesis. It is universal to all species to find their waste offensive." Anders squatted at the water's edge and scooped a sample into a cup, which he then poured into a rectangular device which had been hanging on his belt. "I see. There are several things building up which are likely to be detectable by smell. Would you recognize molecular models of them?"

"Not me," answered Tom. He was beginning to feel a little out of the conversation, and he swam out as far as he could to leave dealing with Anders to Tock.

Tock was excited. "No, I wouldn't either. But I'd love to see them."

"Just a minute," Anders answered. "I'll synthesize the likeliest stuff for you to check by smell, and while that's working I'll show you the models." He tapped on buttons of the face of the synthesizer and Tock experienced a stab of envy.

"I have to tell you, Doctor. At times I'd give a lot for digits like yours." Tock gestured with his nose toward Anders' hands and smiled warmly to take the edge out of what had been a sharp comment. Anders looked at him curiously and sat down to be closer to eye level.

"It is unusual to find a species with your intelligence without means for fine manipulation of the environment."

"That's where I come in," called Tom, waving his fingers in the air to show off his clever hands. "Just tell me what to do."

Anders glanced at him and seemed to dismiss him. "Is that a slave race?" He asked Tock almost as if Tom hadn't been in the same room.

"No!" Tock was shocked at the suggestion. "We depend on the green people to be our hands and they cooperate with us, so that we can make things together."

"It's fun," Tom explained warmly. He wasn't sure he liked this Anders fellow. He was certainly more genuine than the blue guy, but his interest had a funny quality to it, almost as if they were specimens in a collection.

Anders held out a couple of pages to Tock which the rectangular box had produced. "Here. These are the likely culprits. The captions show you chemical composition in universal code. And the pictures."

"Are three dimensional representations of actual molecules!" Tock exclaimed excitedly. "Fascinating! Look at how they all have similar angles here and here and the topography of the branches is so similar. That must have to do with receptor sites in our anatomies."

"Yes," Anders confirmed. "Have you really never seen such pictures?"

"No, never. Could that thing show me any molecule I wanted to see?"

"Sure. What are you interested in?"

"How about a protein. Big old complicated thing?"

"As long as you know its composition. Here. Put it in yourself." And Anders did something that both Tock and Tom somehow knew was monumental. He held the machine down in front of Tock and let him tap in the information using his nose. Anders' big, blunt fingers required a large input system, so by being careful Tock could use it with good precision. Tom swum over and watched while Tock, slowly, at first, figured out which buttons stood for which symbols, and tentatively entered the information.

"We never thought of that," Tom said, as if to himself. "All these years and we just make things to fit our hands." His hands, even with their webbing, were much more delicate than Anders'. He wondered how life might have been different, if Tock and his people didn't need the greens as much.

For his part, Tock was alight with excitement. "Look, poddy, look," he insisted. "This is what that molecule looks like, the one implicated in deepwater seizures." Some of the dolphin people were prone to brain damage after quick ascents from great depths. The inherited condition might not show up for years, until it had been passed on, and it seemed to involve oxygen carrying capacity in the blood. Tom looked at the picture.

"It looks complicated." He offered. He didn't know what to say, really.

"It sure does," Tock remained fascinated. "Look at all that topography. This thing has to function almost mechanically in the bloodstream, you know? It's probably just some minor defect that causes all the trouble." And then to Anders, "How could I get one of these to take back with me?"

The squat man grunted thoughtfully and looked long and hard at Tock. "Perhaps I will give you this one. I'll come back to visit again after the next sleep."

"Of course. That would be great," Tock responded warmly. Anders seemed enthusiastic, too, in his detached way. Tom felt a little left out, but he was glad for his friend. The box made a noise and produced three small packets. Anders tore one open and held it out to them to smell. Nothing.

Used to helping out, Tom picked up the next packet and opened it more carefully. This was the culprit.

"Pew!" Both of them turned away from his outstretched hand. Anders retrieved the offensive sample from Tom's extended fingers and emptied it into the synthesizer. "Here. Try the last one," he urged. "It may contribute to the problem." He was trying to hand the last packet to Tock, and when Tom reached out and took it, Anders looked vaguely surprised.

"Not much," Tom said about the smell. "What do you think?" He held it for Tock, who sniffed it a couple of times and considered before saying, "Right. Not much. Maybe low tide on a hot day." Tom checked again himself and nodded agreement.

"It's not really offensive," Tock explained. "But it's not an attractive smell. If you can eliminate it along with the second one, we should be fine."

Anders poured it into the synthesizer and started working with the machine. Tock and Tom both watched him curiously. He seemed so intent. Finally he looked up.

"Done," he exclaimed, speaking only to Tock. "The climatic controls for your environment have been adjusted. You should begin to detect a change for the better very quickly. In any event, I'll be back to visit again. I want the head of the Planet 483 delegation to meet you. Anything else before I go?"

It was Tom who answered. "Yes. How did your home get its name? Planet 483?" When there was no immediate answer, he explained. "I mean, don't most peoples call their planets something that means home to them?"

Anders shifted his attention somewhat stiffly to Tom. "We are more objective. Ours is the four hundred and eighty-third planet from the mass-center of our galaxy."

"Do you have oceans?" Tom asked.

"Yes," Anders answered. Then he added the all important but unrequested information, "But no intelligent species in them. You're the first water dwellers I've seen. Anything else?"

"No, thank you. And thank you for your help." Tom tied to smile and sound friendly. He was grateful and remotely glad that Anders' planet might be a candidate in their quest, but he felt lonely and a little frightened, too.

XVI

The New Job

AMANDA WATCHED David trot over to greet the screener at the edge of the practice field and realized that it made her feel vaguely lonely and unsettled to know he was talking to someone else. She might have fought for years to have his intelligence generally acknowledged, but that didn't mean she actually wanted to share him, she thought wryly. She sighed and squared her shoulders and walked through the sandy soil to join them.

"Hey, there. How's it going?" She asked.

"Very well in general," the screener answered. There was a definite oddness to talking with a shifting pattern of lights amid an amorphous impression of waviness, but the screener seemed so comfortable somehow and so easy to talk to that Amanda and David both considered it their friend.

"What an interesting setting you've made here," the screener commented. "It's mostly in shades of brown like the two of you."

Amanda chuckled. "I never thought of that, but you're right. It's a recreation of some scrub land near where I was born."

"With the rocks and bushes in all the right places instead of in the way," David added.

"I don't get to see much beyond the teams' quarters." The screener sounded wistful.

"So this is a special visit," Amanda noted. "How come we rate?"

"There's a problem they want us to help with," David told her. Amanda leaned against him and started braiding and unbraiding strands of his mane while they talked.

"Well, not a problem, exactly," the screener qualified. "More of a complication."

"Something about people's agendas, I think," said David.

"Yes," said the screener. It got a little brighter as it hovered near them. Even though it had no face and was too formless to be said to make any gestures, they could tell it was looking at them both. They listened attentively. "It turns out that a number of teams have secondary reasons for coming to these games. Well, 'secondary' may be the wrong word. Sometimes the competition itself is secondary to some other goal."

"Like my quest to have David's intelligence recognized?" Amanda asked.

"Exactly," answered the screener.

"Are people lying to participate?" David asked.

"Oh, no," the screener reassured them. "So far there's nothing nefarious in the least. It's more a matter of trying to help them further their interests without its interfering with the games. Understanding what they want, making introductions, that sort of thing."

"Let me guess," Amanda ventured. "You want David because he's so receptive."

"And you because of your diplomatic skill." Amanda and David both laughed.

"Diplomatic? I wish my brother were here! He'd gasp in shock. He thinks I have the tact of a bulldozer."

"She is blunt," David said.

"Ah, but diplomacy requires much more than what you are calling tact." The screener made a quick decision not to mention Amanda's growing ability to hear and send thoughts at will. She was not yet comfortable with her sensitivity. Instead he emphasized another strength. "You know the concierge? The blue person who showed you to your quarters?" David snorted. Amanda nodded guardedly. "He's very careful in his language, very careful not to offend," the screener continued. "In fact, he's so squeamish about being offensive he manages to get on everybody's nerves." They smiled in recognition. "Amanda, on the other hand, doesn't care much whether people like her."

"You got that right," she agreed laughingly.

"But she cares very much about liking others and she tries to identify with them, even if they're quite different from her. Quite different." The screener paused and the silence stretched out while they considered the implications of this.

Finally David spoke. "And she's willing to work hard for what's right. To work hard for people who may not be able to speak up for themselves." This was the only time he had ever acknowledged all she had done for him, the years of fighting and the long estrangement from her brother. David had always acted as if her crusade were completely hers, and it had been. He had certainly never requested or encouraged it. But he had felt touched and grateful for her feisty, endless love. Now that she had won, he could tell her so.

Amanda couldn't look at him, and her voice sounded tight with emotion. "We'd be glad to be useful. However you think will work."

"Good." The screener was all brisk and business-like. "This is just a function the organizers hadn't known we would need. I'll be in touch to let you know who needs a visit. I knew I could count on you. I don't think it will cut into your practice time too much."

"Don't worry," David said. "We could use about five times the practice they give us. The rest of the time we're cooped up in that room."

"Yeah," Amanda confirmed. "We are not used to being indoors like this. It would be great to have somewhere to go and a chore to do when we can't have access to the practice area."

The screener seemed to focus on them for a moment. "This is a common complaint, this business of being indoors. We've made note of it for future reference. Well, I'm off. See you later." With that it zipped off toward the entryway of the practice space, becoming harder and harder to see.

Suddenly David lurched slightly and pushed Amanda rudely with his rump. "Hey!" She yelled. It got the screener's attention, as David had hoped.

"Would you like to watch us practice?" He called, casting a questioning eye toward Amanda, who agreed immediately with the invitation.

"You said you didn't get to see much, and it wouldn't take long," she persuaded. The screener had approached them again.

"Why thank you," it said, obviously surprised and grateful. "I'm so much busier than I'd thought I'd be, I'll be lucky to attend the finals, let alone any of the preliminaries."

David and Amanda got down to business, moving off toward the largest boulder on their course. "That spin was way too choppy before. Let's start again. Remount practice. Just in case." She directed.

"From the standing sequence on," David agreed. He trotted away, happy to be doing what they did best. Amanda disappeared behind the boulder, then climbed it to stand tall at its highest point. David began to gallop in from the side.

Just as he passed she jumped into a tuck, somersaulting lightly to a standing position on his back. Their routine continued through a long section in which she stood, the horse circling with metronomic precision, so that she could adjust the spring in her knees exactly to his gait and dance on his back as if she'd been standing on firm ground. Finally, she dropped lightly onto his back and he slid smoothly to a stop in the soft earth.

Moving directly toward the screener David took two paces forward leading with his left forefoot high, switched to lead with his right foot and switched back, as if dancing himself to unheard music. He settled back on one pivot foot and started to walk sideways in front. This was the spin she had complained about, an old cowboy move they had reinvented because they liked the pattern it left in the dirt, a circle with a mark in the center. While Amanda held tight with her knees he went faster and faster till his tail and mane and her unruly mop stood out to the side.

He stopped suddenly, facing the screener and slowly bowed down on one knee, lowering his head. As her perch sloped forward Amanda put her own head down and somersaulted spine to spine into a push-off, landing next to him to bow herself. The screener glowed brighter than they had seen. "Bravo!" It exclaimed. "Thank you so much!"

XVII

The Question

JULA WAS VERY grateful for the appearance, if you could call it that, of the screener. She had about had it with the smarmy blue creature who was serving as her welcoming committee. No, she didn't particularly like her room, which was too small. No, she didn't want to attend a dinner and meet other participants in the freestyle. Yes, she wanted to be left alone to sleep, but she hadn't been asked that and she just knew that if she tried to say it, she'd sound as hostile as she felt.

The screener sparkled near the entrance and said, "That's fine, concierge. You may leave us. We'll be fine." He sounded amused. Jula was glad. She could use a little humor, or maybe a lot if she wasn't going to get to sleep soon. To her relief her blues settled softly on her skin and she began to feel their soothing warmth.

"I'm sorry," she said to them. "I've been upset for the last day and a half, haven't I?" The blues hugged just a fraction tighter.

"I hope you don't mind my asking," the screener said. "Were you addressing the butterflies?"

"Yes," Jula answered. "They respond to my mood, my state of mind. When we found out – there's a potential ecological problem on my world, human-caused." She blushed with shame to have to admit that part, and the blues stirred again. "Anyway, I thought I'd have to miss the games because of it and then we made good time and my friend decided..." She trailed off. "Well, here I am. Long trip. Not enough sleep."

"I do understand," the screener offered. "You'd be asleep right now if I weren't here, but it seemed best to visit you now, since you have to start competing right away tomorrow."

Jula nodded. "So what do you need to know? The blues are non-verbal, so if you have a quiz or something, you have to ask me." Now that the dreaded screening was here, she was too tired to care.

"No quiz," the screener chuckled. "I can make contact over a very wide spectrum. But I am having difficulty getting a fix on them. I've already sent for an assistant. He should be here soon."

"What kind of fix do you have to get?" Jula asked.

"I need to make sure they have a separate consciousness, a will of their own, so to speak. The rules of these games call for cooperation between potentially independent intelligent species, which rules out symbiosis or dependency." She looked curious still, so he went on. "They could be a kind of lens that simply enhanced your own contribution to any effort, and that wouldn't qualify."

Jula nodded. "They make up some of my choreography."

The entryway made a chiming sound like the communicators of Jula's planet and the screener heard David say, "All right. I'm here. I wish you would let me in so I can turn off this unfortunate device."

The screener opened the entry and Jula was amazed to have a large brown horse trot in. The room, which had been cozy, was now tiny.

"Is this your assistant?" She blurted.

David fixed her with an intelligent eye and tested her receptivity. "How about making use of one of those appendages you humans are so proud of and turning off this thing around my neck." Jula reached out and flipped the only obvious switch on the thick collar around David's neck. He sighed deeply and rippled his skin all over with pleasure.

"Did I do the right thing?" Jula asked.

"Yes," David answered her then turned to the screener. "This thing does work. I can't hear anybody while I've got it on. It even dulls the sensation on my skin, but I have to tell you that hardly feels safe."

"Spoken like a prey animal," the screener responded understandingly. "Sorry, it's the best I've got. At least it'll keep you from overloading."

"Are you supposed to figure out my blues?' Jula asked David.

For answer he reached out his nose and whuffled softly at her arm. The blues moved slightly with his intake of breath and Jula held out her hand to let him sniff them more closely.

"They want to dance," David reported. "Well, actually, they want her to sleep and then they want to dance."

"Yes, I get that," agreed the screener. Can you read her well enough to hear them separately?"

"Yes. I think so. They are faint." He closed his eyes and exhaled a long breath. Some of the blues actually flew onto his nose. Jula was startled.

"Hey, that's not my doing. They'll go where I send them, but I wasn't sending them."

"Relax," the screener suggested. The unspoken message was to be quiet and Jula caught on. All the times she had worried about some sort of test to make it into the games, but she had certainly never imagined being sniffed by some horse. The oddness of the whole situation struck her; then her worry about the planet surged again, and she didn't know whether to laugh or cry.

David breathed deeply a couple more times then opened his eyes and raised his head. The blues returned to Jula's hand. "How about showing me some of your moves," David asked.

Jula did not feel this message was directed to her, so she waited and a sequence formed in her mind. Slowly she raised her left leg high and to the side, where the blues extended past it and beyond her right arm stretched high for balance. She left her leg immobile and collapsed backward to place her hands on the floor behind her, lifting the other leg to a full handstand with a split. Finally she did battements in the air as the blues formed a braid above her feet, almost as if she were weaving with them. To close she folded neatly to a ball covered in blue, then let the blues appear to pull her up to standing a bit at a time as if she were their puppet. The whole thing had taken about a minute and maybe two square feet of floor space, but it had managed somehow to be musical, elegant, athletic and playful in that small space and time.

The screener made a low whistling noise, unmistakably appreciation. David said, "They are separate from her. They don't have much initiative, but some, and they love to have things be pretty."

"Thank you," the screener responded . "They still seem to me to be connected elsewhere. It may be that they have some shared consciousness with another entity back home."

"No other entity I know of," Jula said, feeling oddly that she should just keep her mouth shut. "I mean, it's a newly settled world, no known intelligent species or we wouldn't have been allowed to pioneer it." There it was! If the blues really were an intelligent species they shouldn't have been allowed to pioneer their world. No wonder she'd been so afraid of not qualifying. She felt tears well up in her eyes.

"Ah, yes. No known species. That's been a repeated mistake, hasn't it?" The screener remarked mildly. He and David seemed to confer a moment and the screener continued. "I do think your blues are part of a larger whole, but there is nothing in our rules precluding such an arrangement."

"Can you tell me anything about it? This other entity?" Jula decided she had passed through too-tired-to-talk into too-tired-to-be-quiet. David riffled the air pensively through his nostrils but offered nothing. The screener expanded and contracted slightly with the effect of a shrug.

"Benign. Could be very large. Likes humans. Fascinated by human babies."

Jula laughed. "Okay. I'll pass that on. Do we pass?'

The screener smiled. Jula was sure it did, though she could never, ever afterward explain how she knew that. Then it answered gently, "Oh, yes. All is well."

"Now, not to be rude," Jula went on, "but I am asleep on my feet."

"Right, of course." The entry opened and David managed to back out, the screener following.

"Oh, wait, I almost forgot," David called. "My shield." Jula flipped it back on and retired to her bed. The last thing she heard was David's voice in her head saying, "Sleep well, both of you. Dance well tomorrow."

XVIII

Now Or Never

Cor looked down at the fitfully sleeping Josh. He decided he would risk snipping the cord that bit into Josh's wrists. Already they had started to bleed and Josh was too sick to lie still so that it wouldn't tighten further. Cor bent down and bit delicately through the cord. Josh groaned and slumped from his side onto his back, almost rolling into Cor.

"Rab, Auntie Rab," he raved in his sleep. Cor bent down again to shush him. They mustn't arouse the soldiers sleeping on the other side of the rocks. The lieutenant already mistrusted him and treated him insolently. But Josh wouldn't hush. He opened glassy, unseeing eyes.

"I'm cold, Rab. Take me under your wing. Please, Auntie Rab."

"Hush! It's Cor, not Rab. Be quiet!"

"Please, Rab," Josh wheedled like a little boy. "Your wings are so soft and warm and I'm so cold."

To shut him up Cor crouched a bit lower, spread a wing over him and cooed softly as his mother would have. "Be still, Josh," he begged.

"I'm so thirsty, Rab." At least Josh's voice was softer. Cor felt miserable. It had been one of the hardest things he'd ever done to eat and drink with the other soldiers that night while Josh, a member of his feeding circle as long as he could remember, went hungry. He wanted to scream with how wrong it all was.

"I know, Joshie, I know. You rest now. Sleep. Just sleep. You'll feel better in the morning." Josh curled up to be under Cor's wing as much as possible and seemed quieter. Suddenly Cor sprawled forward from a hard kick to the middle of his back.

"What the hell is going on?!" The lieutenant spat at him over Josh. Cor stumbled awkwardly to his feet. The lieutenant had his right talons up ready to fight, but he wasn't talking loudly enough to wake the others.

Cor hissed, "The prisoner is sick."

"Of course he's sick. You've seen guano fever before. If he's not dead by morning, he'll be fine. Who are you?!" Josh was blearily awake and half aware that the lieutenant meant no good. As he leaned forward Josh said, "No!" and grabbed the falcon's leg and pushed up to tip him over. Cor flew into them both. He slammed the sick Josh out of the way and grappled with the lieutenant. Talons locked, they struggled in the dirt, writhing to keep their eyes and necks from each others' snapping beaks.

Josh sat up shivering to watch. It was impossible to know how much he understood of what was happening. Maybe he thought he and Cor were still youngsters, ganging up to best a playground foe the way they had countless times, always winning, no marks on anyone to alarm the parents. When the lieutenant spread a wing along the ground to try to push up, Josh said, "Pin him, Cor," and sat on it. Cor took another minute or two of heaving struggle to spread the other wing, but soon they had the exhausted bird pinned to the ground unable to fight.

With his first breath, Cor whispered hoarsely, "Don't move, Joshie, just don't move." And Josh nodded before sinking his head miserably onto his arms.

With his next breath Cor addressed the lieutenant. "Why haven't you called for help?"

"Who are you?!" The lieutenant spat back. When Cor said nothing, he continued, interrupting himself for gasps of air. "You're both big and healthy, but you didn't even take an officer's share of the food. And he was glad to see you. Glad! There's no vengelust there. Who are you?!"

Cor had no idea why he did what he did next. He was desperate and he knew how easily the lieutenant could alread have gotten them both killed. "We are Cor and Josh. We were raised in peace, raised as brothers. We have been trying to get to the port to be transported to the intergalactic games. We fly together. Our people want us to represent this planet."

"Your people?! How many of you are there?"

"Thousands. Three thousand in our town alone." Cor felt better with every sentence, as if a weight were lifting.

"Where? It's not possible. No, don't tell me. Thousands? Living in peace?"

"Yes. Peace and prosperity."

"What do you eat?"

Cor laughed. "We've discovered high protein fungi that we farm underground."

"Farmers?!" The lieutenant's contempt was like a stink, but Cor nearly chuckled again.

"Farmers, hunters, scientists, teachers, artists. Anything is possible when you're not enslaved by killing." The lieutenant fixed him with a stare and was obviously working hard to make sense of all this. Cor tried to help. "You must have guessed at who we are. Wasn't it something like what I'm saying?"

"No, not like that. Thousands. There are stories. Legends. We're told to make fun of them, as if they were made up by cowards."

Cor nodded. "You wouldn't want people hoping for a decent life of peace. Could undermine the war effort."

Josh stirred to life, raising his head. His eyes looked worse and his voice was a harsh croak, "Is that you, Cor? I feel so cold."

"I know, Josh. Whisper, okay?" Then to the lieutenant, "Look, I need to take care of him. Can we let you up? We'll tell you whatever you want to know."

"Why would you take care of him?" The lieutenant asked in bafflement.

"He is part of my feeding circle. Ever since I was a nestling," Cor answered simply. The lieutenant stared at him as if he were crazy. Cor just returned the gaze, steady and strong in the truth.

Slowly, something in the lieutenant seemed to crumble, till he turned his head aside. "You can let me up. I won't do anything."

And he didn't interfere as Cor went over to Josh and pulled him close under one wing. Maybe it was the tenderness of that gesture. So many times the lieutenant had wanted to do this for a dying comrade, but the code of combat forbade such kindness. Maybe it was the low cooing Cor made to comfort Josh, a wonderful sound the lieutenant could not remember ever hearing before. But he found he could not look away from Cor and Josh.

And as Josh stopped shivering and finally fell into a restful sleep, the lieutenant cried. He could not believe he was doing it, but he cried. Cor looked up at him and saw it and the lieutenant didn't even try to hide it. "I want to help you," he said.

XIX

The Dilemma

TOM DIDN'T TRY to stop crying from the shock of the news, but he did keep trying to talk to Tock. "Look, poddy. They just want to help you. You can't say no like that. It's too good an offer." Tock sloshed back and forth at the deep end of their quarters. Tom sprawled in the shallows, for once in his life not feeling energetic. Amanda squatted where Anders had last been.

"It's a real offer, anyway," she said. "They mean it. You'll have to decide for youself whether it's good enough."

"Tell me again what they said," Tock asked.

"The people of planet 483 extend an invitation to the dolphin people to live on our planet," Amanda recited. "The green people are not welcome."

Tock swam up to Tom and beached himself on top of his friend's resting arm. Tock looked just miserable. "I have no idea what to do," he said. "I never thought of this. Ever. I just assumed..." The silence stretched out.

Finally, Amanda spoke. "Maybe you don't do anything, not right now. I can go back to them and say thank you very much; he's considering your offer. Meanwhile we'll set up other meetings. There are still two other teams interested in talking with you."

"You don't think they'll be offended and take the offer back?" Tock asked. He felt equally worried that they would and outraged at what they were suggesting.

Amanda hadn't thought of the possibility of losing the offer. "Hmph. I don't know. I don't have any sense of how easy they are to offend."

"What could they be thinking?" Tock almost wailed. Amanda shifted around uncomfortably and he realized she knew more than she was saying. "You heard stuff? What?" She glanced at Tom, who had stopped crying but still managed to look miserable despite his unexpressive features. He just met her gaze.

"Don't worry," he said. "We greens are hard to offend. Besides I know what they're thinking probably. We're not smart, so they don't want to bother with us."

Amanda nodded. "It is sort of like that," she said. "What I overheard was that they found you unstimulating, so there's no point in having you around and it's bound to destabilize their ecology somewhat to introduce anybody, so why bother with two instead of one."

"Unstimulating?" Tock mused.

"Yes. They seemed to think you found them as stimulating as they found you. Does that make sense to you?"

"Yes." Tock answered grimly. He knew just what they were talking about. He had felt incredibly excited talking to Anders, manipulating his machine even without hands. And when he had let himself imagine living on this planet with a number rather than a name, he had dreamed that Anders' people would invent all kinds of ways for the dolphin race to use tools. The prospect was thrilling beyond belief. But he had never imagined having to leave the green people behind.

"You're right," he told Amanda. "I have to think about this. Maybe I shouldn't even decide. Maybe I should get in touch with the Council back home."

"You could," Amanda agreed skeptically. "It's pretty expensive to do it fast."

"I think we're supposed to decide, poddy," Tom offered surprisingly. "Remember how Oshi treated us and how she said it took so long to choose us?" Tock remembered vividly. They had never discussed it, but the whole thing had given him the willies. "I don't think it would take that long just to pick a couple of nice guys who can wavedance," Tom concluded.

Tock looked miserably at Amanda. She could tell how desperately it weighed on him, how frantic his thinking was growing.

"Let's get practical," she offered decisively. "I'm sure they'd love it back home if you could resolve everything, but for now at least we have the next step. I'll go tell Anders you have to think about the offer, and maybe say you had never considered moving without the green people." Tock nodded enthusiastically. "And then," Amanda continued, "we'll set up the meetings with the others as soon as they can fit in everyone's practice schedule. You guys swimming soon?"

"I don't know," Tom answered. It was the first time since their arrival that he had lost track of the next swim. He pushed Tock familiarly off his arm, went over to the wall and fiddled with various spots till a screen appeared with a schedule. He made it large enough for them all to read.

Amanda pointed. "You're next. Oh, then me and David. I better get back. Here's the plan. I'll go get your meetings set up while you practice, so when you're done, check again. You know how to call me if you need me, right?"

"Right." Tom seemed a little cheered by her can-do tone. The prospect of a good hard swim didn't hurt any either. "You're good at this stuff, Amanda."

She made a face. "Diplomacy?!"

Tom laughed. "Maybe. I don't really know about that, though. I just meant you're a good friend."

Tock looked at his poddy and at Amanda and marveled. Leave it to a green to be appreciative of the person who brought bad news, because they genuinely wanted to help. "I agree," he added.

"Thank you," she said and really meant it. For the first time in her life she thought about her brother's work, so often off on different worlds, and wondered if it might be based in something good, like being a friend.

XX

The Reunion

AMANDA'S BROTHER Asa, Ambassador for the Interplanetary Authority, looked up from scratching David's withers when she entered their quarters. "Hi. I was just trying to make friends," he offered a bit sheepishly.

"Looks like you succeeded," Amanda answered.

David had lowered his head in total relaxation. He exhaled noisily, cocked one forefoot and closed his eyes. "I turned this thing off," the Ambassador continued. David was still wearing the collar-like device for protecting him from others' thoughts. "At least I think I did. It seemed like the right thing to do." Asa stopped in a welter of self-consciousness and doubt completely uncharacteristic of him. A tall, strikingly handsome man, he usually took command by his very presence. David flipped his head briefly to one side and the ambassador correctly read this gesture as a reminder of the itchy withers.

For once Amanda did not find her brother's embarrassment around her pathetic. In fact, she was deeply glad to see him and decided to say so. "This is great, having you here."

They grinned shyly at each other and she walked over to the porch outside her tiny bedroom. "Have you met Aspirin?" She asked, picking up the cat and sitting in the rocker the cat had been warming.

"Aspirin? Like the medicine?"

"Yeah, David and I both think cats were invented to make us feel better." Aspirin stretched elegantly on Amanda's lap and rearranged herself into a tidy circle for sleep.

David had chuckled audibly to Amanda as she introduced the cat and now the Ambassador looked at him oddly. "It occurs to me," he said stiffly, "that he has a sense of humor."

"He does. Stick around another ten years and maybe you'll be able to hear him like me." She hadn't meant to refer to his constant comings and goings, but her remark hit a guilty nerve.

"I certainly haven't stuck around much in the past, have I?" Asa admitted.

"Well," Amanda searched for something true yet unpainful to say. "You must have been around enough. You designed this place, didn't you?"

He actually blushed and looked very pleased. "They interviewed me to figure out how to put you up. They thought a lot of the teams would be pretty homesick."

"Yes, utterly! All of them! At least the ones I've met, and I've met a lot now." And she told him a bit about the farmers who wanted to find customers for their high protein fruit and the water people looking for a new home. Then David told her about Jula and she told the ambassador.

"This is stellar," he declared. "You two seem to have a bit of a sideline going in intergalactic diplomacy."

Amanda groaned so loudly she scared Aspirin and David snorted. He could have sworn that he and Asa shared a laugh over her discomfort.

"Oh, I almost forgot," Amanda recovered. "I do need to do some scheduling to finish making the introductions I promised."

"Mind if I use my cubicle while you work?" Her brother asked. He fished a thin square out of his pocket and held it up.

"Be my guest." Amanda turned toward the wall and opened her scheduling screen. The Ambassador held the square to his forehead and created a kind of semi-opaque helmet-like bubble over his head and shoulders. David could tell he was talking off and on and it looked as if he might be reading something on the inside of the helmet now and again, but the whole thing was way too muffled and out of focus to make any sense. He could also tell that the bubble kept Asa's thoughts completely unreadable, not even the usual blur with occasional words.

David became fuzzily aware of a low rumbly sound and a feeling of affection. He caught a movement to one side and realized Aspirin had jumped onto his fence and was mincing forward, purring and smiling, hoping to smooth her whiskers against his big soft nose. David obliged her by leaning forward and she rubbed one side and then the other against his muzzle. He loved the way her purring tickled and his lower lip quivered with pleasure. He was so glad sometimes to have no hands. Just look how much better his life was than theirs.

Amanda finished and settled back to rock and to watch the horse and the cat. She missed the sun of home and the breeze, the smell of the air. But she was glad, all in all, that they'd come to the games. The Ambassador shut off his cubicle and put it back in his pocket. He looked troubled.

"What is it, brother?" She hadn't called him that in years, but it sounded good. David heard distinctly what the ambassador thought: "I don't want her to know." Then, "yes, I do." The rest was spotty, though he got enough from the Ambassador and from Amanda's questions to grasp the situation.

Josh and Cor had made it to the port, where they had caused a sensation as the first noncombatants ever contacted on their planet. They had been in rough shape, so they'd been given free medical care on a compassionate basis. The pay they offered for transport to the games was uncollectible unless the war ended, so the Interplanetary Authority had almost refused to ship them up, but it would have been rotten publicity not to. The Authority wanted it at least to appear that it was up to somebody else to say the two couldn't compete in the games.

"So somebody knew they were there and was willing to spread the news to make the Authority look heartless?" Amanda asked.

"Yes. That's about right." Her brother was proud of the kinds of questions she was asking and the level of understanding they showed.

"But the Authority is heartless, isn't it? Basically?"

"Well," the Ambassador was clearly uncomfortable. "It's a profit-making governmental body. It can't afford too much heart, but it can't afford too little either. It has to stay around places for years to do business in the black, and if it is perceived as," he hesitated, "unchecked by basic compassion, it will become unwelcome… in places."

"I thought nobody had a choice about welcoming it."

The Ambassador squirmed without actually moving in any way. Amanda had never seen him quite so bothered, and she had tried for years with great success to bother him. "Technically they do have a choice. In practice nobody keeps them away forever because of the benefits of ending isolation. But if the Authority seems to be bad for people, for peoples, its presence can become very difficult to maintain."

Amanda just looked at him in astonishment. She had spent her nearly humanless childhood secure in the knowledge that she was related to one of the most powerful people in all the worlds. She had believed that no matter how distant, enraging and heartbreaking he was, her brother was part of circles so powerful they could not be denied. Now what he was saying was that there were limits even they must acknowledge. She had always imagined she would feel great satisfaction in his being brought down to size, but in fact nothing much seemed to change.

"What are you going to do now that they're here?" She asked.

"That's a problem. They can't compete. The medical care involved prosthetics, so they are altered and we don't have that category in the games. Apparently they make a great interview, though, so they're getting lots of attention, for which they are grateful."

"I'd love to see them fly," Amanda mused.

Her brother made a face. "You and everyone who's heard about them. I just don't know when or how to arrange that."

"How about the closing ceremonies?"

The ambassador was silent for a long moment. "Not in this millennium. Do you have any idea how many people would have to be convinced of that for it to happen?"

XXI

Behind The Scenes

"YOU DON'T HAVE to convince me," Jula told Amanda. "I'd love to see them fly."

"Yeah, but it's turned into this big deal, with the organizers saying we'd be letting the games get used for political purposes." Jula nodded and looked thoughtful. The two girls sat on the floor face to face, each with her feet braced against the other's and her legs stretched wide. The exercise lesson playing on the wall of Jula's room showed two people sitting as they were grasping each other's forearms and bending in wide circles, forward, to the side and back. Amanda thought it looked impossible and said "Ugh," even before they started it.

The next picture involved one of them sitting bent forward over her legs, the other pressing on her back to increase the stretch. Without even having to discuss it they let Amanda, the less supple one, have the first stretch. So her face was squashed into her knees when she heard Jula say, "You know, I can see their point." All Amanda could manage was a muffled "Hmmmph?"

"I'll bet people probably had lots of personal reasons for coming to the games. You know, not just wanting to compete, but wanting to make some other kind of point. Like you and David, wanting to have his intelligence recognized." Another muffled noise came from Amanda. She and Jula had been instant, deepest friends. When they had tried seriously to figure out why, they'd gotten as far as being dancers, being hard to live with, and had collapsed in laughter. Amanda could hardly fathom that they would only have a few more days together before the games ended and they would never see each other again. Meanwhile, this stretch was getting a little long.

Jula continued, "My reason was really political, I guess. Not that I ever thought of it that way before now. But I thought if I did well here, I could go back and go to ground and everybody would accept it. My parent's generation. I wanted everybody to get along. And I'd be the hero of it all." She laughed and released her pressure on Amanda's back, causing a huge groan as Amanda sat up. They switched places, but there wasn't much for Amanda to do. Jula could put her face to the floor between her knees without any assistance, so they continued the conversation with Jula bent in half, Amanda pushing with one hand and massaging her own back with the other.

"Well, that's the way it worked, didn't it?" Asked Amanda. "When the Grounders asked your parents for help putting out the fire?"

"Sort of," Jula answered. "The Grounders got the fire out themselves. They just needed help keeping the Snatchers away. It sounds good back there, but they couldn't afford to send a long text, so I'll find out more when I get home." Jula felt very hopeful, actually, but she kept fighting it down in case there was some kind of new conflict going on. She used one of her mother's phrases, "Many people, many ways to disagree." Amanda smiled. She would remember that one.

The exercise tutorial changed. The two girls stood and faced each other as it showed. They were about the same height, well suited to help each other work out. Jula raised one leg to the side and grabbed her foot, making a triangle of leg, arm and body. Then she placed her free hand on Amanda's shoulder. Amanda reciprocated. The blues flowed warmly over her hand and they actually made her feel a bit steadier. Both girls watched the instruction picture, hoping it wouldn't make them try to do much more in this position. There were a couple of demi-plies, eleves, and the inevitable switch to the other leg to do it all again. Then the picture announced the tutorial's end, and they both sighed with fatigue and slumped down.

"I really appreciate your doing this," Jula said. "You know, even though you're out of the competition."

"Oh, yeah. Of course." Amanda said. "Promise not to tell, but David and I are both relieved about not making the finals. This way we can work harder to get the Peace Team a chance to show their stuff."

"Showing our stuff!" Jula crowed. "That is definitely a fun part of all this."

"And making friends." Amanda agreed.

"And making friends. Even my blues seem to like that. You know, the way they want to touch everybody."

Amanda nodded. She thought something similar might be true for David, too, though he mostly touched others with his mind. "But it stinks being away from home." Amanda offered.

"And being cooped up indoors all the time." Both girls groaned. "And having to eat their gruesome space gravel food." Now they were both laughing hard. "What were we thinking?" Jula shrieked. "This is a disaster!" They laughed so hard they had to sit on Jula's bed, so hard they finally exhausted themselves.

Amanda pointed to Jula's back and asked, "What's the green one for?"

"The green one what?" Amanda couldn't believe Jula didn't know what she was talking about.

"The green butterfly. In the middle of your back." To her astonishment Jula acted as if she'd been stung.

"What?! No! A green one? I don't have any green ones!! Where? I don't see it! Where?" She demanded, all the while pivoting and craning in front of her full-length mirror. Amanda just laughed and turned to the room controls to lower another mirror on the facing wall. As soon as this was done Jula stood like a statue, staring at her back where she could clearly see one of Hank's butterflies.

"It's one of Hank's." She said softly.

"Maybe he wanted to come with you," Amanda offered gently. "Did you leave one of yours with him?"

"No!" Jula declared at once. Her blues fluttered slightly so that they wouldn't be touching her skin. "What do you mean?" She yelled at them. She had never been mad at her blues before. "One of them stayed behind," she told Amanda. "I don't believe it.!" Her outrage deflated to devastation. "Maybe Hank didn't send it. Maybe his greens just sent one by themselves." Her blues settled comfortingly on her and she tried to get what they were telling her. "Hmmph." She blushed.

"What is it?" Amanda demanded.

"They seem to think I couldn't have one of his and he couldn't have one of mine unless we both wanted it."

"Well, well," Amanda teased her. "Somebody's got a honey." Jula glared at her and flopped on the bed again. She didn't want to have a honey.

"I don't know," she said finally. "Do you always know what you want?" Amanda thought about how much she had enjoyed getting to know all the people taking part in the games.

"No," she admitted. "I mean sometimes. Very clearly. Like fighting for David and riding with him. But sometimes I guess I have to find out by trying."

Jula nodded. The two shared a quiet few moments, thinking of what might lie ahead.

"It is really stellar that you made the finals," Amanda said, coming around to the games again.

"I know. It makes me nervous."

"Would you refuse to dance to get the Peace Team into the games?"

Jula groaned. "Stop the competition? You mean a boycott? I'd rather not. There must be another way. You'll find something. Well, I won't say no in stone, but try to figure out something else?"

Amanda sighed. Jula was the third finalist who had struggled through to a reluctant if-all-else-fails on the subject of stopping the games. She really would have to come up with something else.

"You have a petition, right?"

"Nearly unanimous," Amanda confirmed. But she doubted that would prevail. "Somehow the finalists are key. I just don't know how yet."

"You know them all, don't you?" Jula asked.

"Some better than others. I've spent the most time with the water team. You know, those poor guys looking for a planet to adopt them."

"Talk about a political motive for entering," Jula exclaimed. "I wonder why nobody's all in a fuss about them?"

"Maybe it just seems more personal, losing your planet," Amanda offered.

"I don't know. With them and the Peace Team, it's life and death. They both seem pretty personal to me." Jula countered.

Amanda sighed. “It’s just on my mind all the time. Will they get a chance to fly?”

XXII

Getting Off The Ground

"Do you think we'll get the chance to fly?" Josh was talking again. He had had times of not being able to say much ever since they had made it to the port. When Cor had asked him about it, he just said he never imagined getting that far. If anything, he imagined dying at that point. Cor had found it difficult to do some of the interviews with Josh cutting in and out like that.

They sat and perched in their spare small quarters, which actually felt a lot like their cave home to them. One of the teams that didn't use the air had invited them to share their practice space, so they were waiting for their next chance to fly together. Of course, they hadn't been able to do much of their routine so far. Cor tended to panic when they flew together.

At first he had seemed to be the less effected by their experiences of war. He was the one who made contact at the port, agreed to the prosthetics for his wings and Josh's mangled wrists, and tried to establish their credit for the cost of transporting them to the games. He had explained Josh's jumpy distractedness to himself as part of the recovery from guano fever.

Then, that first night they had slept in safety, Cor's own trouble showed. Josh was able to fall asleep immediately, wrapping an arm around Cor as if they were still little boys. Cor relaxed slowly and hard, slept 'like a feather on a windowsill' and woke up with nightmares. Night after night they continued. It got so that Josh would wake him up before he started thrashing really hard and the two of them would talk in the dark, sometimes about what Cor had been dreaming, sometimes about home, sometimes about what had happened on the way to the games, sometimes about all that was happening now. It calmed them. They began to look forward to it.

"The chance to fly in the games?" Cor finally repeated Josh's question. Their daytime conversations tended to be kind of spotty, like this one, with pauses and repetitions that neither of them seemed to mind. "No," he said flatly. "I can't see how they can possibly bend the rules far enough to let us compete."

"Me either," Josh agreed. "Maybe our best hope is some kind of exhibition flight. Sometime. Somehow."

"Hhmm," Cor sounded skeptical. He was beginning to lose confidence. What if he couldn't make it through their routine ever again? How could he even talk about it, when Josh's energy for flying only seemed to grow as time went on?

"What I'd really like is a time to show our stuff when it can be sent far and wide, you know? Like a news show, maybe. One of the ones that have interviewed us."

"You sound so sure of yourself," Cor observed hollowly.

"You know better. I'm just sure of our cause."

Cor sighed and looked away. "What's the matter?" Josh asked gently. "Aren't you? Sure about peace?"

"Yes! Of course I'm sure." Cor surprised himself with his own energy. "After what we saw? Peace is the only hope. It's just... maybe I'm less hopeful. I didn't know... what we were capable of."

Josh moved back as if pushed. "I know. I know. When I was so afraid I had hurt you shooting into the fire, I thought I shouldn't have tried to save the humans. But I wanted to, you know? It didn't occur to me to let them get captured to protect you. And then that whole time in the desert I kept wondering what I would have done if I had known that was my choice, you know? Save them or protect you?" Then his face contorted with the guilt he was going to share, and he almost wailed, "I don't know. I still don't know."

Cor nodded. His eyes were looking deep inside himself. He had his own confession to make. "That night, after I... after they made me..." He couldn't continue.

"When I was sick?" Josh prompted.

Cor nodded and went on, "It was time for feeding and we all just started in. Me, too. I just started, you know?" Josh did know. When somebody who was a part of your feeding circle was absent, you talked about it, all of you, before you ate. You made sure they were okay. And Cor had known he wasn't okay that night. Cor had violated one of the most basic rules that bound them. But that wasn't all. "For a moment, just long enough for that first bite, it seemed right. Just falcons. No humans." He was haunted by the memory of that feeling.

"I know," Josh said very quietly. They were silent then, though the air was almost moving with the energy of their thoughts. Finally, Josh spoke again. "I keep thinking of our parents. How did they do it? They were raised that way! How could they live together after being enemies?"

"My father even served in the army, I think. He won't talk about it," Cor revealed. Josh shook his head in disbelief.

"They are heroes, aren't they?" he asked finally. "And they believe in us. While I was in trouble in the desert back home it felt like a burden that they believe in us so much."

"But now, it's a help," Cor realized. His back straightened and he looked at Josh with some of his old strength and with a new steadiness. "They must have understood we would face… all this. And they believed we'd be able to fly anyway."

"Let's go practice in case we ever get the chance to prove them right," Josh suggested gently. Cor gave a soft version of the call that he would have used to clear the air at home, and the two of them grinned at each other, willing to hope again.

XXIII

The Tide Turns

Tom kept looking for something hopeful to think about, but the best he could come up with was something calming. "It's nothing personal, Tock," Tom explained sadly. He didn't want his poddy mad at the Planet 483 people. After all, nobody made their best decisions when they were mad, and this decision was the most important Tock would ever face. Tock shook his head and frowned.

"I know. I know. They don't mean it that way. That doesn't stop it from meaning something personal to you and me." He swam back and forth a couple of yards at a time, making choppy waves and using up huge amounts of frustrated energy.

"Okay," Tom conceded flatly from his spot in the shallows. He found this whole matter of going to two different planets crushingly sad, and for the first time in his life, the heavy feeling kept returning and his natural lightness couldn't seem to keep him out of it for very long. "It's still nice of them to offer to take you. And the Ludians might want us greens."

They both knew that was a long shot. The Ludians had water problems they were just beginning to tackle and no amount of natural affection for the greens could make up for their planet's physical limitations. Tock grunted in reply and his expressive face showed anger and worry and bafflement.

They had been like this for days. In sheer frustration Tock swam away from Tom, who called after him, "Hey! This is our last practice session. Come back!"

Tock called back to him, "Watch the flocks drill. I'll be back."

Tom sighed, hauled himself partly onto the beach of the practice setting and lay on his back to do as Tock suggested. They had negotiated extra practice time by sharing their setting with the flocks of gulls and seasprites from Sandor who qualified as two organisms on the basis of their intraspecies union. Tom watched the two flocks aim for the same point overhead, flying as hard as they could till the last moment, when they held their wings still and wove among each other like the swift warp and weft on a loom.

He knew how dangerous that maneuver was. He had seen two members of the teams miscalculate, crash in mid-air and fall dead into the water, crumpled feathers and broken necks making them so lifeless it was hard to believe they had just been gloriously airborne.

This time they made it look easy. Tom privately thought their whole routine looked a little too easy, or maybe the right word was predictable. Wavedancers like him and Tock became famous not just for their skills, but for their ability to involve their audiences with infectious fun and risky daring. He and Tock had a name for making people laugh, but he sure didn't feel very funny going into these finals.

The waves preceding Tock's return alerted Tom to his nearness. He slipped back into the water to greet his dolphin friend. "All right. Let's get swimming." But Tock wasn't ready to practice.

"No, wait. I've been thinking. You have to listen to this." Tom felt curious. Something had changed. "There's something wrong with the Planet 483 offer. I've known it from the beginning, but I couldn't think what it was. It's not exactly that they don't want you, it's how they put it."

"All they said was the greens aren't welcome."

"I know! That's just it. That's all they said." Tom did not get what Tock was driving at.

"Maybe that's all they had to say." Tock nodded excitedly, but Tom still felt lost. "I mean they're entitled to their opinion, aren't they?"

"Sure," Tock exulted. "And so are you. And that's what's missing. I don't think it even occurred to them that you would have an opinion or if it did, they didn't care."

"They didn't care." Tom echoed. He knew that wasn't good, and looking into Tock's happy face, he knew it was enough for Tock to turn them down. "But that seems so....simple. Isn't this more complicated than that?"

"That's right!" Tock exulted. "Simple just like you." Tom laughed in spite of himself, but he wasn't convinced this decision would hold.

"Well, that's true. I mean, all of us greens are simple. What are you going to say to them when they ask you if you find us stimulating? They're bound to ask."

Tock rammed him playfully. "I'll say yes!" Tock nearly shouted. "I'll tell them the truth. You are simple. And you stimulate our hearts. And we'll never leave that behind. Never!" He was so happy now that he had decided. Tom caught his giddiness and the two of them played together like a couple of smallfry.

XXIV

Closing Ceremonies

AMANDA FELT GIDDY as she looked out at the spectacle from her spot beside her brother on the stage. She wanted to remember every detail of it forever. She could see David with his protective collar among one group to the left. Most people had stayed with their teammates, but some had come to the awards ceremony individually or with new friends.

She like that phrase, "new friends," and she realized with a thrill that two of the three spots on the awards platform for the freestyle would be filled with new friends of hers. All the other awards and acknowledgements had been given, and this was what everybody had been looking forward to all week. The top three teams would be introduced in the traditional reverse order. Then the giant hall had been configured so that they could each repeat their award-winning performances. The throngs of spectators ringed the sunken stage that could open to reveal any medium and any setting.

Very few people here were not athletes in the games. Most worlds could not afford to send people just to watch. If they were represented at all, it was by service personnel, translators, mechanics, interstellar medics, diplomats like her brother, all people necessary to making the games happen. That meant a notable clot of the blue people who had served as concierges for the event. Amanda shook her head to see that they remained all together, not mingling with the other species much. She would have to talk to Asa about how they had been chosen for their job.

Though only a few thousand were present, all the species in all the galaxies would be watching this event. The Authority had never made such an effort to distribute information so widely and so fast.

"The unexpected success of the games," her brother had called the mass sending.

Amanda felt like a pretty big success herself, even though she and David hadn't made the finals. Come to think of it, she hadn't succeeded in her diplomatic efforts either. Tock and Tom and their peoples still didn't have a new home. Not that they seemed to mind their state of insecurity. Ever since Tock had told Anders no thanks, the lagoon goons had been ebullient. And now Planet 483 was reconsidering, so it wasn't a failure, just not a success yet.

The failure was one she shared with Asa. Neither had been able to wrangle a way for Josh and Cor to fly. Amanda sighed. She wondered if she had done all she could to press their case. She tried to think like her old, furious self, the girl who would have stolen a ship to get her and David to the games. Well, she might not have done that, but she would have had the energy to. She felt all right about her efforts for Josh and Cor. She just wished they had worked. It put a sad note under all the joy of the day.

The music rose, a planetary anthem for the third place finishers, a tall biped and a large felid. Their music had lots of drums, "Lots of heartbeat," Amanda thought as she watched the strong, graceful winners, admirable but so predatory they were almost scary.

Then the music faded and something much airier started up. This was Tock and Tom's music for the second place finish. Everybody loved them and Amanda could trace their progress toward the awards platform by the laughter and cheers. Tock had learned how to spin the floater that carried him in water where others walked and he splashed in all directions as he went, to everyone's delight. After he got his medal, he even splashed the official who awarded it. Tom laughed as hard as anybody else.

By the time that noise died down, the announcement of the first place winner had begun, and the bird-song concerto that was Jula's music began. She approached the platform with less fuss, but there was a collective gasp when, yards away she let her blues fly her up to the first place spot.

Now all three teams were in place and the crowd went wild. The winners bowed and smiled and turned in all directions to include everyone in their triumph. Then they bowed to each other and touched foreheads, the greeting invented by Jula's blues so that they could flow onto others to make contact. It had caught on so fast they were already doing it on the winners' home planets.

As the crowd continued to cheer, Jula called the awards officials over and all five figures on the platform began to talk seriously to them. The chief organizer grew more distressed and finally shook his head no, whereupon all the winners sat down where they were. Or in Tock's case, sank to the bottom of his transparent floater, which had the same effect.

"What's the hold up?" Amanda's brother asked a drab person behind them she guessed must be a security keeper.

"I don't know, sir. Just a minute. They're sending for the screener. I don't know why."

"He can't be in a space like this with so many species, can he?" Asa asked, alarmed for their friend. Amanda's heart began to race with excitement. She was hoping she had guessed what was going on.

"I guess he's going to try." She pointed to the farthest entryway and they watched the screener float in. Silence followed his progress like a wave. "He's probably asking people to be quiet," Amanda guessed. "I hope David can hear him all right with that stupid collar on."

"He'll get someone handed to help him if he needs to," her brother reassured her. Amanda knew he was right.

Then, just as deeply, she knew she had just heard the beginning of something completely new for Earth. Her brother took David's intelligence for granted. She astonished herself by crying several tears, which she just let dribble down. One flowed onto her upper lip and she licked it off. Tears of joy tasted salty, too, she thought.

The silence in the great hall spread until only the rustling of occasional movements occurred. The screener was at the platform and Jula was addressing him, her gestures including the other winners who nodded agreement and spoke some themselves. It was too far away to hear. Finally the screener moved into the performance area, floated upward slightly and seemed to grow a bit larger and more diffuse. He was hard enough to see under much better circumstances.

A quiet but clear voice sounded in every one of the minds present. "Thank you for your cooperation. Please remain silent. The award winning pairs in the freestyle event want to give up their opportunity to perform so that the Peace Team from the planet Ayr can fly." Bedlam erupted. "Please, please. I need your silence. Thank you. They and the officials of the games have agreed that if all assembled here can reach unity on this matter, the Team will fly."

Cheers erupted again, drowning out the poor screener for what seemed like minutes. Amanda noticed that he fell to the floor of the stage and shrank to a small cloud. Finally she heard his voice again. "Please. Silence, please. Thank you. Unity is not the same as enthusiasm. You must be of one will and it must be for the good. You must all silently consider whether the Peace Team should fly, and you will know just as I do if you reach unity. It may take many minutes." And he abruptly stopped talking.

You must be of one will and it must be for the good. Amanda noticed that the silence deepened. She thought about all the arguments she had heard against politics at the games and about how peace on one warring planet was a small matter compared to the wonder of all these species from so many worlds. Her arms felt heavy and still. The silence deepened further, almost as if some flute from a far galaxy were sounding a note too low for anyone to hear. And Amanda thought, peace is what it's all about. What all of this is all about. What could be a better ending to the games?

And like a light going on or a fresh air or an opening up, she felt it. Nothing changed, yet everything did. They reached unity. The screener's voice sounded happy in her mind. "Thank you, friends. They will fly."

And they did fly, Cor with his odd-colored replacement feathers, Josh with new skin and muscle at his wrists. They looked happy but overwhelmed by the cheering as they walked out to the performance area. There was something so ordinary about them, Amanda thought.

As if he had read her mind her brother said out loud, "It is always ordinary people who make the difference." And together all the peoples of the games watched the extraordinary spectacle as Cor lifted Josh from the ground, spiraled upward and the two began their routine. Most who saw it in person that day and those on many worlds agreed. Had they been allowed to compete, Josh and Cor would have won. But nobody really cared about that as much as they cared about the courage and strength they were witnessing.

Many cried. Many tight hearts opened wider. The peace talks on Ayr began soon after as a direct result of their performance, though it was several years before they could safely go home. And as always on all worlds, nobody knew how much had come together to make it all possible.

www.ingramcontent.com/pod-product-compliance
Ingram Content Group UK Ltd.
Pitfield, Milton Keynes, MK11 3LW, UK
UKHW041935190726
13854UKWH00004B/1605